VINYL DESTINATION

Adam Millard is the author of twenty novels, seventeen novellas, and more than two hundred short stories, which can be found in various collections and anthologies. Probably best known for his post-apocalyptic fiction, Adam also writes fantasy/horror for children, as well as bizarro fiction for several publishers. His work has been translated for the German, Spanish, and Russian markets. He lives in Newcastle-under-Lyme with his wife, Dawn, and his two cats, Butter and Toast.

A CIP catalogue record for this book is available from the British Library

ISBN: 978-1-7384764-4-2

Crowded Quarantine Publications
124 Dimsdale Parade Western
Newcastle-Under-Lyme
Staffordshire
ST5 8DU

VINYL DESTINATION

Adam Millard

"One good thing about music, when it hits you, you feel no pain." - Bob Marley

"I sting, but he was worth it." – song from the failed musical, Beauty and the Yeast Infection

1

The truck thundered along the potholed road, indifferent to the terrified cars, cyclists and geriatrics it left in its wake. The driver – a portly fellow, recently divorced, member of a Meat Loaf tribute act – lit a cigarette; a bad habit, but how could he drink and not smoke? The two went together like salt and pepper, Ike and Tina, priests and choirboys...

Ted Butcher was his name; Ted to his friend (not plural), Edward to his parents (whom he'd recently moved back in with), and "wanker" to those he narrowly missed with his unstoppable death-machine. A barrage of horns sounded, signifying the general dissent at Ted's maniacal manoeuvres, but he didn't care; it was damn near impossible to hear them over the stereo, which assured him that he was a bat out of hell, and he'd be gone when the morning comes.

In back was a load of old LPs. Nobody wanted them anymore; the world had progressed so far – so *quickly* – that the systems used to play the obsolete records were no longer even manufactured. Those still extant were kept in peoples' attics or basements, gathering dust or propping up other useless artefacts of bygone eras. Sure, old people still clung to their record players as if they might, one day, make a comeback, but it wasn't going to happen, not with all the fancy-schmancy iPods and *streaming downloads* – whatever the hell *those* were. Those seniors still clinging to their archaic turntables would be dead long before they ever realised how fucking futile their nostalgia was.

Like countless others in his fleet, Ted Butcher was on a mission: it was their job to collect every godforsaken LP in England. They wouldn't get them all, of course; the government had estimated some eighty-thousand records would remain for now, trapped in dingy cellars and back rooms all across England. Only after the homeowners expired would they see the light of day, and then they would be dispersed amongst the thrift shops like a plague; Dusty Springfield and Louis Armstrong cluttering shelves once again, useful only for squashing spiders skittering amongst the other old junk.

Ted still had three more stops to make before his shift was over. Pulling up in front of CARTER & CARTER'S OLDEN DAY BULLSHIT, he ticked another one off his list and climbed down from the cab, singing about being a dead ringer for love, and briskly made his way into the antique shop.

A bell tinkled overhead, announcing his arrival. The smell – olden day bullshit *indeed* – hit him so hard, it took a few moments to compose himself. See, another reason why they'd been sent out to gather up all the records was this: they stank to high hell. Years of disuse had seen their cardboard sleeves rot away, growing stuff that should really only thrive in a rainforest. Why, just earlier that day, Ted had visited a dog pound where they'd been using Roy Orbison's back catalogue to scoop shit out of the kennels. 'Pretty Woman', indeed...

"Ah, you must be Fred," came a jovial voice from his left. Ted turned to the man in tweed mincing towards him. "Come to relieve us of our records."

"It's *Ted*," he replied, "and I assume you've got them all bagged up and ready to go as requested?"

The man's extreme side-part was dreadfully disconcerting. "We have indeed," he said, smiling. Roger and I were up all night. We've got eighteen bags in total, three of those devoted to *The Carpenters Greatest Hits* alone. Some extremely rare tracks in there..."

"Well, they're about to become even rarer," Ted said, glancing around the store. The place was badly cluttered; shelves were lined with dusty old shit that nobody could possibly ever want.

"If you don't mind me asking," the tweed-weed said, "what's going to happen to them? The records, I mean."

"I didn't think you meant The Carpenters," Ted replied, coming off a bit more curt than perhaps he'd intended. As the beginnings of a frown furrowed the proprietor's brow, Ted continued, "They're off to the new landfill, mate. A whole field on the outskirts of town dug up, ready, waiting to feed on Michael Jackson, Belinda Carlisle, Little Pattie, and Jive Bunny."

"That's *terrible*," the man said. "You can't put Little Pattie in the same hole as Michael Jackson."

"Anyway," Ted said. "I'm in a bit of a rush, so if you could point me in the direction of the bags, I'll get loaded up and on my way."

"Yes, yes of course," the man said. He reminded Ted of his old history teacher, Mr. Hill, inasmuch as they were both cunts. "Roger! Roger! The truck's here for the LP harvest!"

Roger appeared in the doorway behind the counter. He was either the tweed-weed's twin brother, or a remarkable clone. "Ah, we've been expecting you," he said, with all the camp of a handbag full of rainbows. "It's not easy, you know, parting with such beautiful music. I cried last night, and a little this morning. To destroy such wondrous things ought to be a crime."

"It's a known fact," Ted said, "that thirty-five percent of recorded suicides in the UK are directly influenced by Coldplay's X&Y album." He didn't know if this statistic were true or not, but it sounded feasible. "If there is just one 12″ version in those bags of yours, then I believe I'm doing my bit as a citizen of Bellbrook." Now that he thought about it, he rather fancied the idea of being a hero. *Maybe I should get Mum to make me a costume...*

"Well, I think it's terrible," Roger said, turning his nose up high enough for Ted to count the hairs within. "It's part of our history they're destroying, Luthor. You wouldn't bury famous paintings, would you?"

As someone who had seen Tracey Emin's last exhibition, Ted would have to answer Roger's question with a resounding *yes*. Bury them, but only after killing them with fire first.

"You'll have to excuse Roger," Luthor apologised. "He's got a flair for the dramatic."

Roger, not to be discouraged, slid across the floor as if on invisible castors. "Judy Garland, Bette Midler, Shakin' Stevens," he sighed, "all buried to slowly decompose... useless... forgotten." The back of his hand somehow found its way to his forehead.

"Actually, it will take decades, *centuries* even, for the records to even begin deteriorating," Ted said. Roger recoiled as the truck driver's pickled breath met his nostrils.

"Oh, I get it," Roger said. "Out of sight, out of mind."

Ted shook his head. "No. Fact is, vinyl makes a great liner for landfills. The LPs will be pressed down and covered in all manner of crap. You see, they can't melt 'em down – too many harsh chemicals – and since they're about as degradable as Joan Rivers' face, they're putting 'em to good use instead."

"Hear that, Roger?" Luthor said, forcing a smile. "It's not like they'll be going to waste or anything."

"No, they'll be buried beneath a load of shit," Roger quipped. "So *much* better."

"Look," Ted said, glancing down at his naked wrist (he hadn't worn a watch in years). "Can we just get the bags loaded up already? It'll be dark soon, and I'm having fish-fingers for tea."

"Come on then," Roger said, his dejection apparent. "The sooner they're gone, the sooner I can start the mourning process."

Ted sniggered, catching himself only after realising that the poor, deluded fellow was deadly serious.

2

The excavation was done, for the day at least, and all thanks to the strange structure they'd unearthed at the bottom of the pit. Like something out of Lovecraft's wettest, wildest dreams, the edifice seemed to glare at the crew up above, the bulk of which had ceased work to see what all the fuss was about.

"What is it?" O'Brian asked. The hand-rolled cigarette in the corner of his mouth bounced up and down as he spoke. "Some sort of *crypt*?"

"In Bellbrook?" Kavannah, the foreman, replied incredulously. "You've got more chance of it being a stray pyramid."

"I don't like the look of it, Kav," Dennis said as he climbed down from his digger. "You read about things like this in the paper. Before you know it, people are dropping down dead in the middle of the street. Does anyone remember that film with the cemetery and the pets in it? You know, the pets and the cemetery? What was that one called?"

O'Brian shrugged. "*All Dogs Go to Heaven*?"

"Look, it's probably just old foundations," Kavannah said. "Get the clay down there and you won't even see that brickwork."

"But, what if it's an ancient, Indian burial ground?" Dennis looked genuinely terrified, and was met with much derision by the rest of the gang. One of the apprentices – a young scrote by the name of Alfie – vomited coffee from his nose.

"Again, in *Bellbrook*?" Kavannah said. "I don't know whether they taught history at your school, mate, but as far as I'm aware, we didn't have many ancient Indians in England, and certainly not enough to create a burial ground for."

"Didn't they find that King under a car-park last year?" O'Brian asked. "Maybe there's another one of 'em down there."

"I think the car-park King was a one-off," Kavannah said, realising how ridiculous he sounded before the words even passed his lips. "Look, I don't want to hear any more stupid speculation about what it is, okay? As far as I'm concerned, we've all got a job to do, and a stack of bricks twenty feet underground ain't gonna give you all the afternoon off."

As he walked away shaking his head – his authority clearly demonstrated to those in the immediate vicinity – the gathered workmen exchanged troubled glances. It wasn't, as their foreman had so eloquently put it, a mere stack of bricks; there was an entire structure down there, large enough to house several families of Iranian refugees. Lord only knew what lie inside, but its ornate design suggested that an otherworldly Hugh Heffner might find himself quite at home within, so long as he had plenty of bizarro bunnies to play with.

"You heard the man," O'Brian said, kicking a clod of dirt into the hole. "Get some clay down there before we all go crazy looking at it."

3

Marcia Martin closed her laptop and went to grab her bag and coat. She was, as always, the last to leave the office; she hated talking to the other writers, columnists and editors at the best of times, and joining them in their scuttle at the end of yet another fruitless day would only incite unwanted conversation. Through experience, she found that leaving it an extra ten, fifteen minutes late ensured that she could avoid such bollocks and simply head home in peace.

"Hey Marcia," someone said, startling her. She looked up to find Clarence Jameson leaning against her desk, as if auditioning for the next office calendar.

Clarence; that steaming pile of sleaze had been harassing her for over half a year already. From the very moment she'd taken her job at the paper, he'd been all over her like a cheap suit. Repeatedly telling him to *fuck the fuck off* had done nothing to convince him of her disinterest; if anything, he'd only upped his game, finally resorting to hitting on her after the rest of the office had dispersed.

"Clarence," she exhaled. "You startled me. I thought I was the only one left."

He grinned. "Yeah, you did," he said, which would have creeped out most women, but not Marcia; she'd long since grown accustomed to his tactless nature.

"So, what can I do for you?" she asked, regretting it instantly. Images of what she *could* do for him were no doubt already coursing through his perverted mind. She watched as the corners of his mouth edged slightly upwards; she half expected his tongue to flick out at her.

"I just thought I'd walk you to your car," he said. "Perhaps we could go over that nursing home story for tomorrow's edition. I *did* take the photos for it. Who would have thought it? My name on top of yours in an article; on top of yours. Me... on top of y—"

"Yeah, I get it," Marcia interrupted. Her flesh was now crawling. "And I don't need an escort, Clarence." *Now fuck off, you creepy sonofabitch.*

"You're not lesbian, are you?" Clarence asked. "I mean, I consider myself a sex magician, but I doubt I can do anything about *that*." He smiled sheepishly, as if his nuts were retracting and he was fighting to keep them out.

Marcia, sensing an opportunity that might never present itself again, replied: "Well, I do like looking through lingerie catalogues, and I'm ever so fond of Natasha Henstridge films…" It was her turn to smile. She nibbled at her lower lip, as if the mere thought of *Species 2* had ignited something long-dormant within her.

Clarence drummed his fingers along the edge of her desk. "Yeah, that sounds about right. I'd been wondering how you could resist me; should have known you were a muncher from the start." He rolled his eyes and smiled. "And on that note, I'll see you tomorrow." His schoolboy satchel bounced upon his arse as he turned and made for the lift.

Marcia was amazed by how quickly he'd lost interest, cursing herself for not thinking of this tactic sooner. *Six months!* Six whole months of sleaze and double entendres, and all she'd had to do was profess her (disingenuous) love of the fairer sex.

With a smug smile, she slung her purse across her shoulder and headed off for the stairs.

4

"Is this the last of it?" the foreman asked. How did Ted know he was foreman? Well, he was wearing a Hi-Vis waistcoat, and the man just had that *look* about him. The chewing gum he perpetually grazed upon only confirmed it.

Ted climbed down from the cab of his truck. "Yeah, this is the last one. Where do you want it?"

"In that bloody great hole would be good," the foreman said, somewhat tersely. Ted couldn't help feeling that he was being wronged for something this poor fucker's crew had done that day. Maybe he wasn't getting any at home; perhaps he was annoyed at the slivers of grey peppering his beard, or the fact that his face sagged a little to the left, like some stroke victim on horse tranquillizers.

"What, you really want me to start offloading now?" Ted asked. It was awfully hard not to sound incredulous.

The foreman sighed before glancing at his watch. After almost ten seconds (yeah, he was definitely in charge here) he said: "It's getting late. Do you have to clock out? I can get one of the lackeys to put this lot in before they piss off home."

Ted nodded his approval. "Cheers. I'm having fish-fingers for tea."

"That's... *irrelevant*," the foreman said, gesturing to one of his underlings, who came scampering like some hunchbacked thing from an old black-and-white movie. "Alfie, I want you to get the rest of these records down there before you go home."

"Will I get overtime?" Alfie asked, wiping his acne-pocked nose on the back of his sleeve.

The foreman gritted his teeth. "You'll get a job tomorrow, and the day after, and the day after..." Ted didn't stick around to hear the rest; he already had an idea how the rest of their conversation would play out, and his cab wasn't going to unhook itself.

As he worked, he thought about the Carter brothers and their olden day bullshit; he thought about the piles of *Grease* soundtracks, Debbie Harry singles, and all the Prince and Marillion albums he'd collected over the course of the day, but mainly (drooling as he whistled about what he wouldn't do for love) he thought about his mother handing him a plate of breaded cod and a mound of buttered bread.

5

Darkness, *wondrous* darkness; the kind of darkness you might wish for in the midst of a particularly keen migraine, which was exactly what the thing in the pit had been suffering ever since those inconsiderate bastards had shown up with their Day-Glo vests and constant banter over who had the largest penis.

How *dare* they! With their intricate digging machines and lack of personal hygiene. Just who did they think they were? You wouldn't kick a wasp's nest and then stand around for the next week casually chatting about who would win in a fight, Ricky Gervais or Karl Pilkington. You wouldn't break into a lion enclosure and then spend the next few days hawking greenies in their feline faces, which was pretty much what these bozos had been doing since they'd appeared, like assholes from another dimension, a week earlier.

Ah, but now they were gone, and silence reigned once again (well, apart from some hobo in the distance spouting religious nonsense at the top of his tobacco-parched lungs). It was blissful.

It had been sleeping, lying dormant, for longer than it could remember. Despite having infinite fingers, it couldn't, for the life of it, count the years it had been slumbering. Centuries? Millennia? If you were to tell the thing down at the bottom of that pit it had napped through forty-two presidential inaugurations, eight British coronations, sixteen popes and three number ones by the Danish pop group, Aqua, it would have told you to stop talking nonsense and shut the fuck up. It had slept, somewhat peacefully, through Emmet's Insurrection, Janissaries' Revolt, the Mormon War, World War I and II, Vietnam, and even the Great War of Blur Vs. Oasis. It had nearly been roused when "Little Boy" rocked Hiroshima, like a noisy neighbour downstairs, but after smacking its lips and rolling over, it had been slumbering ever since.

And now, this; twenty pricks in garish costume had unearthed it – the equivalent of pulling someone's duvet off on a winter's morn.

How fucking rude, it thought.

And to top it all off, the crazy bastards had replaced the good old mud and general earth with some sort of hard, black shit. Some of it was sheathed in colourful wrapping; some of it not. There appeared to be images on the packaging: men with ridiculous hairstyles and bizarre instruments; barely-dressed women in suggestive poses, mounting things, licking things, and being largely uncouth.

Some things had certainly changed.

After pondering the subject for a while, the thing in the pit realised it had two choices: it could attempt to go back to sleep; perhaps the anger would subside, and darkness would return in all its splendour, rendering it unconscious, once again, for another few centuries. Or – the much more tempting prospect – it could teach those little fuckers up there a lesson. They had unceremoniously awakened it, dumped a massive load of shit onto its head, and simply waltzed off into the night as if they hadn't a care in the world.

Well, I suppose I could pop up there for a little bit, the Pit-Dweller thought, stretching its innumerable invisible limbs. And as it pushed upward, kicking off of its mausoleum and the forgotten city beneath, something strange and unexpected happened: a sound echoed through its mind. No, not a *sound*; music. A *song*, even. Something about... love... *love*... and how it's all you need...

Whatever, the thing thought as it flew off into the night, dispersing, giving itself to the winds. Still, no matter how hard it tried, it just couldn't get that blasted song out of its head.

6

Ted stared down at his plate in disbelief. *Must be some sort of joke*, he thought, nudging one of the sausages with his fork. Finally, he had to speak up.

"Mum, I thought it was fish-finger night? I've been telling everyone at work I was having fish-fingers and…" He jabbed a sausage and waved it in the air, as if signalling an aircraft. "…fucking *sausages*, Mum."

"Don't you talk to your mother like that," said his father, Bill Butcher. "And there's nothing wrong with those sausages. While you're under our roof, you'll eat what *we* put on the table. Did you talk to that ex-missus of yours like that?"

"She never lied about fish-finger night," Ted said, dropping the fork onto his plate. "And anyway I don't have much choice at the moment. I'll be out of your hair as soon as I get some money together."

"Money?" Edith Butcher spat. "You've never had money, Edward. Not even when you were married to that cheating whore of yours."

Ted sighed. "Can we not call her names?"

"Says 'em how I sees 'em," Edith said. "Would you prefer prostitute? Harlot? Streetwalker? H—"

"Hoe?" Bill offered.

"I was just about to say hoe," Edith said, patting her husband's head. He looked up from his plate and smiled at her.

"I would prefer if we didn't talk about her at all," Ted said, glancing down at the sausage and finding it even more disgusting, given the direction the conversation had taken.

"Bad day at work?" Bill asked, sucking gravy from a sausage as if it were a...

"You could say that," Ted said, trying not to make eye contact with his deep-throating father. "Do you know how many people still have LPs?"

"I think it's terrible," Edith said, peppering her mashed potato as if it had somehow wronged her. "Throwing away good music like that just doesn't make any *sense* to me. There would be uproar if people started doing that with books."

"I think it's a good idea," said Bill. "Think about all the space they've cleared. All those lofts gasping, not knowing what to do with all that clean air. Did you know that you are now seventy percent less likely to die from a collapsing attic than you were before the LP harvest?"

"Where did you read that nonsense?" Edith said.

"It's *not* nonsense," Bill replied. "It's *science*. And our boy here is on the front line, making Bellbrook a safer place for everyone. Sure, the townsfolk might think he's a cunt, but he's the cunt that saved their lives."

"Thanks, Dad," Ted said, failing to feign appreciation. "And we got *most* of them, I think," he added. It was impossible to get every single LP in Bellbrook, but he'd given it his best. There would always be those sad, unfortunate souls, reluctant to move on, unable to allow technological advancements into their life, and good luck to them. You never saw them complaining about technology when they needed a pacemaker fitting...

"Well, I don't like it," Edith said, forking mash into her face. When she next spoke, a geyser of potato spewed forth. "This country's gone mad. First it was the smoking ban, then the pissing-in-the-park ban, and now this."

"*What* pissing-in-the-park ban?" Ted asked, incredulous.

"You know," Edith said; they really didn't. "You can't piss in the park anymore. Why, twice last week the police threatened to arrest me."

"You've *never* been allowed to piss in the park!" Ted said, pinching his nose between his thumb and forefinger. All of a sudden, he had a terrible headache. "Mum, please tell me you're joking."

After a second or two of silence, Edith Butcher grinned. "Of *course* I am," she lied. "Pissing in the park, indeed." She made a mental note not to mention the shitting-at-the-zoo incident either.

"What your mother is trying to say," Bill said, "is that she's too old and stubborn to accept that times, they are a-changing."

Edith Butcher's jaw dropped so far, it nearly landed in the mountain of spuds before her. "I'm not *old*," she gasped, "I just think that—"

They never did find out what she thought, as the house began to tremble violently before she could finish her sentence. Cutlery clattered from the drawers; plates fell and shattered on the lino, forming a sea of porcelain shards that would have given a sadomasochist a raging erection. Edith rose from her saet – or at least that's what she was going for when she toppled backwards, taking the tablecloth and all that sat upon it with her.

This wouldn't be happening if we'd had fish-fingers, Ted thought as he hit the deck. An antique radio set – replete with dials and switches that no one knew how to work anymore – tipped over and landed on the back of his head, knocking his vision sideways.

Bill got up and launched himself at the door, not expecting the refrigerator to meet him halfway there. His body slammed into it with such force that his dentures flew from his mouth and landed somewhere behind the cooker.

The tremor lasted under a minute all told, but by the time it finally passed, the kitchen was in complete disarray. Most homes in Bellbrook had been built long before earthquakes ever became a concern, and the bombsite that had (up until a moment ago) been a perfectly respectable dining room proved that even its smallest shitholes were in desperate need of a universal upgrade.

"Wha da sham ell wash at?" Bill just about managed through slack, tremulous lips.

Ted clambered to his feet, glancing down at the radio that had almost bashed his skull in. "Quake?" he offered, rubbing the back of his head.

Edith, wearing three dinners and six rounds of bread and butter, appeared somewhat dazed and confused. "But we don't *have* earthquakes in this country," she countered. "The government banned them back in 2010."

"Wall, tha wash defenly one," Bill said. "Ya didin happena shee whar ma teesh wen, dijoo?"

7

Marcia Martin had just poured herself a large glass of rosé and was about to start editing a piece on local dog-grooming services when the quake suddenly struck, knocking her straight out of her chair. Picking herself up off the carpet, she sniffed at the air.

Something was burning…

It didn't take long to determine what, however; her laptop lie beside her in a smoking heap, shooting sparks. The article she'd been working on, which had been titled ROOM FOR A GROOM BOOM, would unfortunately never see the light of day.

She was just about to call her mother, who lived across town in a residential home, when the phone suddenly rang. Thankfully it was still in the same room as her, judging by the sound of it, and after a few rings she was able to locate it and answer.

"Hello?"

"Marcia! Are you okay?"

Grimacing, she replied, "Clarence, why are you calling?"

"Well, at first I was going to call about the whole lesbian thing, and how we could work around it, but then everything started to shake, so I thought I'd better check on that fine ass of yours either way." He was breathless, which was new; he was also tactless, which wasn't.

"Clarence, do you have any idea how misogynistic you are?"

"Thanks," he said.

"It wasn't a compliment, and FYI," she continued, "up until a moment ago, I was quite happily munching carpet..." – not a lie – "...and I sincerely doubt that even you, with all your charisma and film-star looks..." – *Hatchet II* – "...could make me straight." She was almost starting to believe her own bullshit. Pretty soon she'd be hitting strip clubs and watching *Loose Women*.

"Whose rug were you munching?" asked Clarence, sounding positively depraved. "It's Carol from advertising, isn't it? She must be the butch—"

Marcia promptly hung up and dialled Sunnyville Residential Home.

Those poor people, she thought. They only had four good hips between them *before* the quake...

8

Gladys Moore snatched the phone from its cradle and blew the dust from the mouthpiece.

"Yeah?" she answered

"It's Marcia Martin."

"That's nice," Gladys said. "Look, I've got a whole load of mangled old people here, and I don't—"

"I'm ringing to check on my mother, Vera Martin?"

The home manager's tone changed instantly – and unsurprisingly – once she realised who she was speaking to. "Oh! Erm, Vera's *fine*. In fact, she slept through the whole thing!"

The voice on the line didn't sound entirely convinced of its own story.

"Slept *through*... can I speak with her, please?"

Gladys rolled her eyes. "Ms. Martin, I can *assure* you that everything's fine; there have been no deaths, at least not since the quake, and your mother will call you back in the morning, once we've got the place settled and untangled everyone."

"Look, if you don't put my mother on this minute, I'm going to write a strongly worded letter to my MP, and then write a nice article of defamation for the newspaper I work for. Do. I. Make. My. Self. Clear?"

Gladys gave the receiver the finger before replying, "I'll just go fetch her then, Ms. Martin. Please bear with me."

9

Marcia waited for the cantankerous old trout to return with her mother, listening closely as she did. A strange, steady rumble could be heard in the distance, interposed by the much louder noise of passing sirens. Whatever was causing this bedlam out there, it terrified Marcia to her very core.

Were there more quakes yet to come? Was this the end of the world? Had the Mayans been right, give or take a few years? Something wholly unnatural was happening; something, Marcia thought, *big*.

"Marcia?"

The voice was so unexpected that she almost dropped the phone. Following a brief juggle, she forced it to her ear once again. "Oh, mother, are you *okay*? Is everything *alright*? You're not hurt, are you?"

"I'm alright, love," her mother said. "Just a few bumps. We were just settling in to watch that nice man on the telly. You know; the orange man that does the antiques? What was it, dear; an earthquake?"

Marcia sighed as relief washed over her. "Yeah, I think so," she said, though for all she knew some overzealous despot had finally dropped a bomb, and the faint roar she heard was, in fact, the subsequent fireball making its way toward Bellbrook.

There would have been a flash, she reminded herself, though what she knew about nuclear weapons she had learnt from *When The Wind Blows* and Stanley Kubrick films.

"And are *you* okay?" her mother asked. "You sound a bit upset."

"I'm fine," she lied. "I was just worried about you—"

A hearty, old-lady chuckle crackled through the receiver; Marcia smiled. "You don't have to worry about me, love," her mother said. "I've been on this Earth too long to let one of Mother Nature's little farts frighten me. Look, I've got to go, dear. Mrs. Moore's giving me funny looks through the window... now she's rolling her eyes... yep, she wants me to hang up..."

"Okay, mother," Marcia said. "And do me a favour, will you? If they're not treating you right there, tell me."

"Oh, dear, I like it here. Mrs. Moore's *okay*, really, and we all like to play little tricks on her. Like yesterday, she confiscated Albert Matlock's harmonica because he kept playing Al Jolson tunes over and over, so we covered her toilet seat with cling-film. It works both ways, dear." She chortled.

"Give her hell," Marcia laughed. "And Mum..."

"Yes dear?"

"I love you."

"I love you too, dear."

As Marcia hung up, sirens wailed past her flat outside. The ominous roar, which had initially terrified her, had already been reduced to little more than background noise by this point. She glanced around the room, which looked like the aftermath of a Czechoslovakian gang bang, and simply said, "Fuck."

10

"Did you see his face?" Lee Jones asked, sipping cider from the can in his shoddily tattooed hand. "Do you need new pants, Alf?"

"Yeah, y-yeah, A-Alfie," Calvin Broome added in his own inimitable way. "Your f-face was a p-picture." His stutter was the icing on an already shitty cake: parrot-nose, wonky eyes, and breath so bad his doctor prescribed him tic-tacs.

"Whatever," Alfie said, brushing the dirt off his jeans. "Dudes, you've gotta admit, that was one pretty bad quake."

Lee shook his head and pulled another can from its plastic ring. "That was nothing," he said, trying to sound insightful and brave, and failing with aplomb.

"N-nothing," Calvin agreed, sipping nervously from his 3% lager and hopping from one foot to the other as if the ground beneath him might suddenly open and swallow him whole. "Th-that was n-nothing, A-Alf."

Surprisingly, the bus stop had retained all its window panes. Crudely doodled penises and vaginas rattled upon the glass as the tremor dissipated, but somehow they had not shattered in the quake.

"Look, I've got work in the morning," Alfie said, thinking about the landfill site. "I'm not staying out much longer."

"He's scared," Lee snorted, laughing. "It was only a fucking earthquake, ya pussy."

"Y-yeah, ya p-pussy."

"I'm not scared," Alfie protested. "I know what it was. I've just got to be up early is all, and standing around a bus stop all night isn't exactly my idea of fun."

Lee emptied the contents of his can into his mouth, crushed it with his gnarly fingers, and said, "We're not standing here all night; I've got an idea."

"H-he's got a f-fucking g-great i-idea," Calvin added, hopping up and down in place. His uncharacteristic excitement worried Alfie.

"Come on, scaredy-cat," Lee said, stepping out into the night. "We're not gonna let a little earthquake stop us from having a bit of fun."

Alfie sighed, lit a cigarette – which his mother would smell on him later and berate him for – and followed his mates along Barker Street, all the time staring at the ground, watching for cracks that weren't there.

11

The Pit-Dweller hadn't meant to fart, and it certainly hadn't expected its flatulence to be forceful enough to knock the whole town off its feet. Still, better out than in; that's what happens when you're cooped up underground for several centuries.

Soaring up into the atmosphere, the vengeful entity grew more and more intent on wreaking as much havoc as inhumanly possible. *Eye for eye, tooth for tooth, hand for hand, foot for foot*; the thing remember the passage from Exodus. But there was another line in its ethereal mind, a piece certainly not from the Bible:

...Fuck that shit, 'cause I ain't the one, for a punk motherfucker with a badge and a gun...

What could it mean? Where did it *come* from? The thing was utterly perplexed, so much so that it took all its focus just to keep floating upward, reaching an altitude where it could properly unleash upon the townsfolk far below. It hadn't meant to kill anyone initially; simply teach them a little respect for their world, their planet, and the things that dwelt within it. But now, somehow, something had changed. It *wanted* to kill them, and it was going to have a bloody fun time doing it.

Yes. *Fun.* A concept it didn't understand, yet there it was. Girls just wanna have it; it's good in the summertime.

Fun, Fun, Fun; a word so nice The Beach Boys used it thrice...

What the hell is wrong with me? the Pit-Dweller thought. *And who the fuck are The Beach Boys?*

Without any further ado, the thing glanced down at the town of Bellbrook and grinned – at least it would have had it been a physical entity, and not a wraith-like ball of sheer malevolence.

Goodness gracious great balls of fire, it thought, having no idea why.

It spread itself out, an otherworldly miasma descending upon the town, infusing its environs with evil spirit. No one would escape its touch, and all would suffer...

Suffer little children...

The thing sniggered sinisterly on its way down.

12

Leroy slapped her again, and again, and one last time, just in case the first two had been too soft. She didn't cry – they never did – but he could see that she was angry, with him, and with herself for letting him get away with it.

"What do you say?" he said, raising his hand as if to strike her a fourth time.

"I'm sorry," she sighed. "It won't happen again."

Leroy lowered his hand which, if he was honest, stung like a sonofabitch. "That's what I'm talking 'bout, gyal. I like you, Sonja, but you'd best not let me catch you fucking without my permission again, d'ya hear me?"

She nodded. Unfortunately, she heard him just fine. "Won't happen again, Leroy," she said. She checked her nose for blood, but she knew there wouldn't be any; he would never beat her too hard, not if he expected her to keep working for him. And hardly anyone liked fucking girls that looked like they'd already been run over, anyway.

"Now, gyal, get back to work. Dat earthquake ting is done and dusted, and I don't fink you's quite ready to clock off jus' yet, ya feel me?"

"I feel you, Leroy," Sonja said.

"Good." He slapped her on the arse and it was, she thought, the hardest of the four. "You can do two more punters before midnight, and den come and find me. If I's in good mood, I let you finish."

As he bounced off down the street, Sonja watched, praying that something terrible would befall him by the end of the night. If someone could just set his afro on fire, she thought, that would be great, or attack him for the sole purpose of stealing all his jewellery. There were fifteen Cash4Gold outlets in Bellbrook alone, after all.

She hoped for another quake, one that would swallow the prick up for good.

Sonja walked slowly along the sidewalk, surprised to find headlights flashing her before she'd even taken six steps. She made for the car as it slowed down and pulled over, feeling something whoosh past her as she did. The stench of rotting shit and musty paper filled her nostrils momentarily, but faded just as quickly as it came.

Forgetting the strange occurrence almost immediately, she smiled, put on her best whore walk, and continued toward the punter who'd put her halfway to her nightly quota.

13

"You gots to be firm wid dem gyals," Leroy muttered. He found his best conversations were those he had with himself. "Dem gyals like it. Treat 'em mean, keep 'em fuckin' for a livin'."

He'd been a pimp for most of his life. There had been a few months, back when he was twenty, when he'd attempted to clean up his act. He'd waited tables at Nando's on weekends, stood in men's toilets with a bottle of soap, a tray of condoms, and an array of cheap aftershaves to force upon patrons in exchange for paltry tips. He'd even worked as a telesales rep, flogging life insurance to people that were never going to die, not in his lifetime. In the end though, old tricks died hard, and by the age of twenty-one, he'd collected five new women and was making more money than he'd ever earned serving chicken or convincing teenagers that they'd most likely catch something terminal by age thirty.

Pimping was his game, and the man had no shame. Leroy was so good at it that he had a waiting list longer than George Michael's charge-sheet. Hoes were queuing up to become a part of his team, and not just because he offered a retirement plan and every second Sunday off.

He kept the bad dogs at bay, and the one thing these bitches needed was security. They knew that if they went to him with a complaint – a punter going too far, putting things where they didn't belong, refusing to pay, kissing on the lips, paying in Drachma – he'd take care of it. He was what they called in the trade: a bad motherfucker. He even had a embroidered wallet identifying him as such. Sure, Samuel L. Jackson had it first, but the title applied to him equally as well.

It had been a nice night thus far, despite that passing rumble. The only thing that could possibly drag him down was an impromptu stop by the pigs. There were sirens in the distance, and as far as Leroy was concerned, that was the best place for them.

"Dyam quake done shook up da town," he mumbled, surveying the debris all around. A lamp-post had fallen over in his path. Stepping over it, he was just about to reach for his cigarettes when something very strange happened.

His mind went completely blank. It was almost as if everything he'd learnt, from his humble birth to ascending the throne of Bellbrook's top pimp, had been instantaneously expunged from his brain. He just stood there with his hand in his jacket pocket; Lord knows what he'd been reaching for. Whatever it was, it no longer seemed important. What *was* important, however, was the strange urge presently coursing through him; a desire he could no more control than he could suddenly will himself to perform brain surgery.

What he felt was an overwhelming compulsion to *dance*.

Now, Leroy just wasn't a dancer. He'd avoided discos and bars with dance floors for the simple reason that people might mistake his spasmodic jiving for an extreme case of epilepsy.

And yet, here he was, standing on a darkened street corner with dance surging through him like an itch that desperately needed to be scratched. And not just any dance, but something demanding, moves that were liable to put him in the hospital, an entire ballet of bone-breaking manoeuvres he had no idea how to perform properly.

"Dyam shizzle," he grunted. It took all he had just to say those words, and they weren't even words inasmuch as you wouldn't find them in the Scrabble dictionary, no matter how hard you looked.

His right leg suddenly popped out, and before he knew what was happening, the left went in the opposite direction.

And then...

...he was dancing; thrashing about the pavement as if he were under attack by a swarm of invisible wasps. His arms flailed all around, seemingly independent of his body. He was like a marionette *sans* strings, and if he wasn't careful, he was liable to do some serious damage to himself and his immediate surroundings.

"Da fuck?" he said, legs performing a little two-step without warning. He then began to twirl around in a circle, and even as his stomach threatened to expel the hotdogs he'd consumed for dinner, he twirled and twirled some more. His mind reeled and his entire body ached, and he finally understood why Michael Flatley had ultimately gone insane.

A car drifted slowly past the dancing lunatic; its driver honked the horn, turned up the stereo, as if the music would somehow help him. "You GO, you crazy sonofabitch!" the motorist yelled through his open window.

"Fo shizzle my nizzle," Leroy said. Even the words weren't his own, or the voice for that matter. His deep, sonorous tone was completely gone, replaced by a high-pitched, nasally whine that would've had Prince reaching for his junk to check that everything was present and accounted for.

As the car drove off, taking with it the screeching dubstep that sounded like two Transformers fucking, Leroy dropped to his knees.

What's happening to me? asked the terrified voice inside his head, the one he still recognised as his own. "I'm a slave to the rhythm, a slave to the rhythm, a slave to the rhythm of loooooooove!" the shrill imposter belted out, just before Leroy finally lost his lunch.

14

"Sharon Conker reports from outside Knickers Nightclub. Sharon, what can you tell us about the earthquake Bellbrook experienced mere moments ago?"

Marcia turned to face the telly; she hated Sharon Conker with a passion, but there was always the chance she might fuck up live on air. *Let this be it,* she thought. *If there is a God, now's the time to prove it and give that belligerent, venomous young twat a stroke.*

"We've got reports coming in from all over the town," the alleged reporter began, flipping her hair like she was auditioning for a *Pantene* advert. "It's still too early to tell just how much damage this quake has caused, but it's been confirmed that several people were squashed to death when the statue of William Bellbrook, our town's founder, fell from its plinth. We also have one reported death from Sunnyville Residential Home…"

Marcia's heart leapt into her mouth.

"…but it appears that the body belonging to Mabel Perry had been dead for almost a week already, and had simply been overlooked by staff."

Marcia relaxed, somewhat.

"Have we learned the epicentre of this particular quake?" the invisible anchor asked. *"I mean, earthquakes are not usually our sort of thing, are they? We're lucky to get a nice flood; maybe a forty-mph wind in October."*

"That's right," Sharon said. "Bellbrook is not known for its earth-shakers, but let us not forget that we're only five thousand or so miles from Los Angeles, and six thousand from Fukushima. It may be that one of their quakes fancied a change of scenery. I mean, let's face it, we're all connected, aren't we? Who decides where these things happen?"

"Tectonic plates?" Marcia offered, incredulous.

"Indeed," the anchor said. *"I can see you have your hands full there, Sharon. Is there any particular reason why you're outside Knickers Nightclub?"*

On the screen, a group of unruly revellers were leaping all about behind the reporter, pulling their pants down to expose arse-cracks and shouting things in a language that could only be described as drunkenese.

"Tonight, Knickers is hosting a very special party," Sharon said. "And we have it on good authority that several celebs are already inside, nestled in the VIP area."

The invisible anchor chortled in response. *"Boy, they've sure picked the wrong night to sample the delights Bellbrook has to offer."*

"They certainly have," Sharon said, following up with a laugh marginally faker than her tan. Marcia reached for the remote; if this was the embodiment of inspired reporting, she wanted nothing more to do with it. "Michael J. Fox, Tara Reid, Professor Stephen Hawking, that guy from *Scrubs*, and Marilyn Monroe, they're all inside Knickers right now, drinking the place dry..."

"Sharon, I'm pretty sure Marilyn Monroe died a while back?" the anchor said, making his statement sound like a question. God forbid he make her look like a *complete* ass on live TV.

Sharon pushed a perfectly manicured finger into her ear, pretending there was something wrong with the connection. "Haha," she said. "You mustn't have heard me correctly.

Marilyn *Manson* is inside Knickers tonight; Marilyn Monroe is most certainly still dead."

"She sure is," the anchor replied. *"I'm sure you'll be keeping us up to date with news about this mysterious earthquake as it comes in."*

"Well," Sharon said, gesturing to the Knickers entrance in the background, "as I said, Professor Stephen Hawking is inside right now, downing shots with Tara Reid. I'm hoping to get a few words from him as to what might have caused this anomaly. I mean, if anyone knows about science-y stuff, it's him. Don't let that Dalek voice fool you, people." She then proceeded to mimic the good professor, very badly, which was, the network decided, the perfect time to pull the plug.

"Sharon Conker, reporting from Knickers Nightclub, Bellbrook," the nervous-looking anchor said.

Marcia switched off the telly and poured herself a fifth glass of wine. She simply couldn't believe that anyone – executives so high up, they suffered perpetual nosebleeds – deemed Sharon Conker a competent reporter. While she was in front of the camera, covering *real* stories about things that mattered, Marcia was stuck writing articles about snowboarding squirrels and women in Africa with two vaginas.

It just wasn't *fair.*

Marcia had never wanted to be on TV; there was something about having her face splashed all over the tabloids – and splashed over by those high-up execs – that just didn't appeal to her. But that didn't mean she couldn't report on real stories, too.

Setting down her untouched glass of wine on the coffee table, Marcia got up and got dressed. Reluctantly, she dialled Clarence's number. When he answered, she gave him no time to speak any further than "hello."

"Meet me on High Street in half an hour," she said, then quickly hung up.

There was a story here somewhere; she could feel it in her uterus. Necking the entire glass of wine – Dutch courage – she promptly hit the door, leaving her apartment in the same shit state it would likely remain for quite some time.

15

Sonja had seen some grotesque penises in her time – the oak tree, the mini-mollusc, and the two-headed purple tarantula all came to mind – but as she stared down at the thing protruding from O'Brian's zipper, she felt the sudden urge to quit whoring, move to Scotland, and become a manicurist.

"Something the matter?" O'Brian asked. "It ain't gonna suck itself."

Sonja swallowed something that hadn't been there a moment ago, composed herself as best she could, and said, "Do you mind if I don't?"

"Well, actually," O'Brian said, looking slightly miffed, "I *would* mind, since coin has already changed hands. How would you like it if, say, you came to me and said, 'Hey, Mr. O'Brian, I'm aware that you're one of the best builders in Bellbrook. I need a conservatory knocking up in my back garden, and there's no-one else I'd rather do it than you,' and then, I show up, after you've already paid the reasonably priced invoice, and decide I'd much rather just plonk down a garden shed instead?"

Sonja thought about it for a second; he made a good point. As she considered it, the fleshy thing in her hand seemed to wink at her. "Yeah, I just can't go through with it," she said. "Anything else, though, should be fine." She reached into her bra and produced a small square of paper, unfolding it until it was roughly the size of an ordnance survey map of Russia. She handed it to O'Brian, who now wore the expression of someone not entirely impressed. "Pick any two things from the menu, and I'll do the cheapest one for free. Sound good to you?"

"This is bullshit!" he said, glancing down at the exhaustive list. "All I wanted was a good ol' fashioned bl... *ooh*, I'll *accept* your offer," he said, jabbing an excited finger at

– and through – the prostitute's *carte du jour*. "I'll have a number 26, and a 47. The 26 is *free*?"

"Totally free," she said, sighing with relief – a 26 required minimal touching. Plus, he'd be facing the other way.

"Do you even *have* a deck of cards?" he asked. "I mean, it's not exactly the kind of thing you'd expect a lady of the night to be carrying around in her handbag."

Reaching into her own purse, Sonja produced two decks of cards. "A 26 requires an unopened, unshuffled deck of cards; therefore, by law, we have to carry one at all times. As you can see, I carry not one but *two*, just in case I get a couple of perverts in the same night."

"Ever happened before?" O'Brian asked.

"Never. In fact, I've carried both decks in my bag for nearly ten years. The 26 isn't as popular as you'd think; I think the chance of paper-cuts puts most punters off."

"Not me," O'Brian said with conviction, "let's get cracking." Without another word, he turned his back to her, bared his ass, and buried his head down in the foot-well of his Ford Capri. With his disgusting cock finally out of sight, Sonja relaxed and began to peel the cellophane wrapping from the deck of cards.

It was then that her phone rang. She reached into her bra – yes, prostitutes use these for extra storage; make-up, money, packed lunches (only small things, though, like scotch eggs and brownies) – and pulled out her cell, which (while not the *very* first to roll off the line) looked more like something you'd throw through an enemy's window with a threatening note taped to it than an actual device of communication.

She answered swiftly, cutting off the Pussycat Dolls ringtone before it became too embarrassing. "Hello?"

O'Brian heaved a dramatic sigh. "Is this gonna take long?" he asked. "My ass is getting cold…"

Sonja shushed him as the voice on the line began to speak.

"Yo, woman! Check dis! Be at da muthafuckin' cemetery in fifteen minutes, or yo ass is freelancin', get me?"

It was Leroy all right, but it sure didn't *sound* like the Leroy she knew. His voice was much higher now, as if he'd plaited his balls with elastic bands.

"I'm with a client," she said, studying the flabby, pasty ass beside her. "And what do you *mean*, the cemetery?"

"Did I stutter, Billie Jean? Fifteen, or you'll be fuckin' wid da man in da mirror!" He hung up abruptly, but not before adding, "OOOWWW!!!"

Sonja dropped the phone back into her cleavage. "Well *this* is certainly awkward," she said. For a moment, she considered giving O'Brian's ass a consolatory pat, but quickly thought better of it and drew her hand away. "Sorry, but I've got to go," she said, snatching up her handbag. "I'll leave the cards though, and you can sort yourself out, if you like."

By the time O'Brian had extracted his head from the foot-well, the passenger-side door was swinging on its hinges, and the sound of Sonja's heels had already faded to a distant echo.

"Fucking hell!" he cried. Then he picked up the half-unwrapped deck of cards and smiled. "Ah well, got *me* a date with four queens..."

16

Meanwhile, the Pit-Dweller had spread itself out across the entirety of Bellbrook, blanketing the town with pure, unadulterated evil. In the back of its mind (though not by choice), a choirboy kept warbling on about walking in the air.

If only I could find the mute button, it thought, having no idea what a mute button even was. A stealthy clothes fastener?

Meanwhile, some townsfolk had taken to the streets down below, apparently intrigued by the earth-shaking anomaly that had just ripped through their sleepy little hamlet about an hour ago.

Look at them, the thing thought, *with their silly pyjamas and unkempt hair*. From high above, it looked like a swarm of wild toupees flitting about. *I'll teach them to fuck with me...*

Wisps of its unholy essence tore away and streamed back down to Earth. It watched, laughed, and almost choked as the residents of Bellbrook began to spasm and shake; infected and impregnated by its evil. The thing felt like a modern-day Santa Claus, though instead of delivering presents, it delivered hell, and instead of eating their cookies and drinking their milk, it... well, that was where the comparison ended.

When the choirboy in its head finally stopped singing, the Pit-Dweller heaved a massive sigh of relief. But then Enya came on, and it found itself in two minds whether to aim for the nearest river.

17

Kavannah stood outside his house, wind whipping his face, the strange smell of burnt something-or-other stinging his nostrils. He was still dressed in his workwear; there was really no point in changing, as he'd only have to put it all back on again in the morning. To his mind, he was saving time, effort, and bathwater by simply keeping his overalls on all night. He wasn't a complete scruff, though; the cats would usually lick off a portion of the dirt and grime whenever he returned home.

Standing there in his overalls, with his bright blue safety helmet still perched atop his bald pate, the man looked completely vacant. It was as if somebody had picked him up while he was sleeping, dropped him on the street, slapped him in the face and run off, as quickly as possible, into the night.

Memories were vague and fuzzy at best. He could just about recall the mighty cleaning the cats had given him, right after he'd settled down in front of the telly with a steak-and-kidney pie and a Nebuchadnezzar of cheap cider, but that was about it.

Maybe I'm pissed, a slurred voice said inside his muddled head.

But he'd barely even touched the cider, which, incidentally, was what the brewers had apparently been going for when they'd decided to make it damn near impossible to stomach.

So he couldn't be drunk, but this did nothing to alleviate his fears in the slightest. Something else had led him to stand up from his comfortable armchair, ignore the final three minutes of a particularly complex *Murder She Wrote*, and head outside, where he now found himself, motionless and feeling rather queasy.

Suddenly, an idea that was not his own lit up his befuddled brain. "I'm a construction worker," he mumbled to himself. "What I need to do is find myself a copper, a

Native American chap, a cowboy, a GI, and a man dressed in all black leather."

It made absolutely no sense whatsoever, and yet he was bloody going to do it, even if it took him all night.

A cab swerved around him as he stepped out into the street – *where had that come from?* – hopping the kerb on its opposite side before crashing into a telephone pole.

Kavannah didn't care. If the driver was dead, well, he shouldn't have swerved. Didn't they teach these people anything in driving school?

The driver, rightly irate, climbed out of the wreck and unleashed a torrent of rude words – *what exactly was a cum-jangler, anyway?* – at the dazed idiot stumbling around in the road. Kavannah, not one to be perturbed, turned to the livid bastard and said:

"Mate, if you'll pipe down just a second, I've got a question to ask."

"Pipe dow... he wants me to pipe down. You're lucky I didn't go over you, you daft prick! Go on, then."

Kavannah cleared his throat, straightened his helmet and asked, in all seriousness:

"Where's the closest YMCA?"

18

It was around 9pm by the time Edith Butcher finally managed to get the house back in order. Bill had been cursing for the entire duration, moving things from one place to another, hissing through his gums as the search for his missing dentures continued. It had taken less time to find Josef Fritzl's basement, Ted thought. They were all about ready to give up when his father finally dragged the cooker out.

"Gacha, ya liffle bashardsh!"

"Have you found them, dear?" Edith asked, placing a framed photograph of Penn and Teller back onto the mantelpiece. Quite why they kept a framed photo of the illusionist duo had always been mystery, and Ted had never asked.

Bill gave his teeth the most cursory of blows before immediately stuffing them back into his mouth. He smiled bright and wide, revealing what appeared to be a mouse dropping between his top incisors. Though Ted had never actually seen one before, he could only suppose that this was what they called a shit-eating grin.

It was shortly after that when Bill *really* lost his marbles. One minute he'd been flicking through the TV channels, searching for something that didn't have Ant and Dec on it, and the next he was up, swinging his hips, using Edith's knitting needles to play air guitar. At first, Ted and Edith sat watching, assuming that the man was suffering a simple stroke, but after a few minutes, it became clear that something had gone horribly wrong.

"Dad, you're going to give yourself a hernia...."

Ted lunged out of the way as his father leapt across the room, dislocating one hip and causing the other to make a not-so-reassuring sound – like a twig snapped underfoot, or one of Kate Moss's toes.

"Son, I can't... I can't *help* it. Shit, my knee's busted, and I think I've just... yep, I can feel it running down my leg."

"Bill, just sit down for a minute," Edith said, patting the cushion beside her nonchalantly. "Remember what the doctor said about sudden movements?"

"The doctor doesn't know what he's on about," Bill said, lowering himself down into his own armchair. "Oh, deary me, I've never felt such *pain*."

Ted watched his father from a safe distance, and he couldn't help but notice something else odd about him. Seated in the armchair, with lord only knew dribbling down his shins, was what appeared to be a total stranger. It still bore the face of his father, but it was slimmer somehow, and definitely different. His top lip quivered, lopsided, as if he might sneeze at any moment, and the wrinkles that had previously made up about ninety percent of his face had all but vanish.

"And just what are you gawping at?" the stranger asked, that tremulous lip lifting ever higher, as if someone had fish-hooked it and was now giving a jolly good tug.

Ted didn't answer; he was simply too shocked to speak. Instead, he tapped his passing mother (carrying a sewing kit now, for some reason) on the shoulder.

"Hm?" she said.

"Mum, look at Dad, will you, and tell me if you see anything strange."

"Why, I don't need to *look* at him to tell you that," she said, unpacking bits and bobs and laying them out on the kitchen table, where she always did her crochet, macramé, knitting, stitching, embroidery, doily-making, cheese-cosy sewing, and knicker-elastic repairs. "I'm afraid he hasn't been the same since that nice lady down at the newsagents told him there would be no more *Railway Weekly*. Knocked him about something rotten, that did. Didn't it, Bil—"

She screamed as her gaze fell upon the intruder, seated right where Bill had been only moments before. He was even wearing Bill's dungarees, which could only mean one thing: someone had broken in, killed Bill, disposed of the naked body, climbed into his clothes – which were ill-fitting, to say the least – and plonked himself down in front of the telly.

"Who the *hell* are you?" Edith gasped, grabbing the nearest thing that could be utilised as a weapon, which just so happened to be a ball of crimson wool. The man in the armchair had the knitting needles, however, clicking them together to a familiar beat. Was that *Heartbreak Hotel?*

"What are you going on about, woman," the stranger said. "Have we got another gas leak?"

"B-bill?" she managed, just before fainting. Ted caught her before she hit the floor, but not before the oak table met her head about halfway down.

"What's the matter with her?" the stranger mumbled, looking stranger every second. He'd begun to take on a dull hue, as if all the colour were being drained from his body. Even his clothing was turning monochrome, like an old, faded picture.

"Dad, I think something... *odd* might be happening to you," Ted said, laying his mother's unconscious form upon the sofa. "You've gone all black and white on us." He went off in search of a mirror – well, anything with a reflective surface – and handed him a stainless steel ladle from the kitchen.

Gazing at his own alien likeness, Bill wore the expression of a lost man, confused and terrified, yet oddly intrigued. "I look alright for an old fella," Ted's father finally said. "A little bit on the drab side perhaps, but..."

"Look at your lip!" Ted shouted. "That's not even your *face*. You've been bloody well possessed, that's what. Why else would you thrash about like that, nearly rupturing your spleen? There's a demon inside you, Dad, and his name is fucking Elvis. Elvis Aaron Presley."

Bill glanced at the face in the ladle once again, and though its concavity distorted his countenance, there could be no mistaking the reflection: he was looking at the King of rock and roll himself.

"Holy *shit*! I *am* Elvis!" Bill cried, suddenly leaping up with twice-renewed vigour. He swung his broken hips left, swung his broken hips right, nearly toppling the mail stand in the process. "Is this *real*? Am I *dreaming*?"

Ted shrugged. Unless his mother had laced their sausages with LSD, a dream was the only sensible explanation. But whose dream *was* it, then?

"I feel so damned *young*," not-quite-Bill said. "So... so... what's the word?"

"Freakish?" Ted offered.

"*Virile*," his father countered, "like I could impregnate a woman with just a look and one of these!" He thrust his groin lewdly forward. Ted was thankful his father was wearing dungarees; regular jeans would have been around his ankles by now.

"Mum will be pleased to hear that when she comes round," Ted said. "Dad, we need to get you to a hospital, or something. I think... something really *bad* is happening to you. This black-and-white thing isn't normal, and you've lost nearly five stone in five minutes, which also can't be right..."

"Pfft, hospital schmospital," Bill said. "I haven't felt this alive since The Andrews Sisters invited me back to their hotel room in 1957."

"That never happened, Dad," Ted said, crouching beside his unconscious mother. A snail-trail of drool glistened down her cheek. *I should check she hasn't swallowed her tongue*, he thought. He was just about to pry her mouth open when she suddenly sat bolt upright, mumbling incoherently as she tried to get up.

"Mum, it's okay. Everything's fine. Just relax—"

"I had a terrible nightmare," she gasped, lips quivering and eyes bulging from their sockets. "Your father... he... he was in his chair, only it wasn't *him*. It sounded like him, but it was... and I know this is going to sound silly... it was *Elvis Presley*." Here she took a deep breath and made the sign of the cross.

"Uh-huh," not-quite-Bill said, butting his black-and-white head into the conversation. "Ma'am, do you have any idea how absurd that sounds?"

Edith screamed, and as her eyes rolled back into her head, Ted gently lowered her back onto the couch.

"Was that really necessary?" he asked, turning to find his father gone. Footfalls on the stairs (two at a time, the lithe bastard) told Ted that this night, this strange, terrible night, was about to get much worse. Standing up, his knees audibly protesting beneath him, he couldn't help but pray in vain that this was somehow just a dream after all.

19

"*The hills are aliiiiiiiiive, with the sound of muuuuuuuusiiiiiic...*" sang the nun, barrelling down Frederick Street.

Those queuing outside Knickers Nightclub turned to see what all the fuss was about. There were predictable mumblings about mad nuns and crystal meth as the woman – "*off her tits, she is; that's what happens when religious folk drink cider*" – launched into a somersault, snagging her habit on a Vauxhall Vectra's wheel-trim. The crowd lining the footpath all cheered, encouraging the nun to get up and have another crack at it.

And she probably would have, had a number 59 bus not come along at that exact moment and...

"...shame," one of the spectators said.

"I hope she was a real nun," another one said. "Otherwise, she'll probably be going..." he trailed off, jabbing a thumb down at the pavement.

"Sewers?" a confused woman asked.

From there, the conversation escalated into a debate whether priests, nuns, vicars and popes got preferential treatment in heaven – sort of like a VIP area, but without the free champagne and dancing girls.

"We're not gonna get in," Alfie whispered. They'd almost reached the velvet rope, not to mention the two gargantuan bastards blocking their way. "I'm not even wearing proper shoes."

"Shit," Lee replied, glancing down at Alfie's feet. "Why didn't you say so earlier? And why are you wearing Crocs in the first place?"

"I didn't know we were going to Knickers! I knew this was a bad idea all along..."

"Pity you didn't know Crocs were a bad idea," Lee snorted.

"C-crocs, for f-fu-fuck's sake," Calvin thought to add. "They're f-for s-simpletons and f-five year olds."

"Thanks," Alfie replied, "but that doesn't help us get into Knickers, does it? There's no way Fee-Fi and Fo-Fum are going to let us in. This is stupid anyway. I don't even know who most of these so-called celebrities are."

"Well, Michael J. Fox was big in the eighties," Lee said, "but his career's been a bit... shaky lately. Marilyn Manson, she's just some Yank who wears a lot of black and swears a lot. Tara Reid – yeah, I'm not sure about that one either – but that guy from *Scrubs* is in there. Everyone knows him. And then there's Stephen Hawking, who has something to do with space, I think. My mother fancies him. In fact..." He produced a small, black book from his pocket. "...I'm on a bit of a mission. She says if I get Hawking's autograph, she'll buy me a bottle of whiskey and a quarter ounce of something green and fragrant, and I'm not talking about parsley."

"Are you t-talking about t-thyme?" Calvin asked.

"I thought he was in a wheelchair," Alfie said, as the queue edged ever-so-slightly forward.

"So?" Lee said, tucking the autograph book away. "Doesn't mean he's *totally* lazy. I mean, how much energy does it take to write your name on a piece of paper, anyway?"

The young couple in front of them, who had spent the last ten minutes probing each other's mouths for foreign objects with their tongues, were admitted to the club. The giants blocking the door stepped aside, parting like a pair of thick, ugly curtains. Once the slobbering lovers crossed the threshold, the blockade resumed, and it was the boys' turn to be scrutinized.

"You lads gonna be trouble?" Fee-Fi grunted. He sounded, Alfie thought, like a knackered transit on its last legs.

The boys exchanged nervous glances. Surely one of them would have to say something. When no one else stepped up to the plate, Alfie finally answered, "Not at all. Lee's dad's in the police, ain't he, Lee?"

Lee nodded. It was an impulse response; his father worked at the dirty magazine shop down the subway. "That's right," he lied. "My old man's a copper, and I'm already signed up to join m'self. Got a truncheon test next week to see how hard I can hit."

The doormen shared a conspiratorial glance, one that said: *we don't for a minute believe you, but since you had the balls to concoct such a ridiculous story, we just might let you in anyway, and if you mess up, we'll be the first to jump on you, beat you to within an inch of your life, and drag your sorry asses back out into the street, where you'll spend the remainder of the evening, broken, lying in a puddle of your own piss and vomit.*

"Hang on. Barry, look," Fo-Fum said, pointing at Alfie's feet. "He's wearing bloody Crocs..."

Barry – *Fee-Fi* – looked down at them with disdain. "We have a strict policy against Crocs," he said. "In fact, any footwear with holes in it. Move along, boys."

"B-but h-he's got n-needs," Calvin said, stepping forward. "We all h-have. I've g-got a st-stutter, and Alfie's g-got something wrong w-with his f-feet that means he can only w-wear shoes that allow th-them to b-breathe. If you d-don't let us in b-because w-we're mental, th-then you're g-going to be in a l-lot of t-trouble. W-we're here to see one of our k-kind. Y-you might have h-heard of h-him; a science-y guy? Goes b-by the name of P-Professor H-Hawking?"

What the hell are you playing at? Alfie thought, though he had to admit it was just crazy enough to possibly work.

Fee-Fi grimaced as if he'd been whacked in the nuts with the hardcover edition of *A Brief History of Time*; Fo-Fum simply stood there, scratching his head. The folks in line behind them continued to mutter amongst themselves, and meanwhile a paramedic had arrived on scene to collect what was left of the singing nun. Eventually, Fo-Fum said:

"Alright, but if I catch any of you cunts whacking off over Tara Reid in there, I'm gonna show you what a steel-toed boot feels like – up your arse."

With that he stepped aside, and Fee-Fi followed suit.

"Thanks," Lee said, stepping past them.

"Ta," Alfie muttered, trying his damnedest not to make eye contact.

"R-really ap-appreciate it, g-guys," Calvin said. When they were out of earshot, Fee-Fi turned to Fo-Fum and said:

"Why's it always the stutterers that talk the most?"

20

It was cold, damp, and windy in the cemetery, and, Sonja thought, full of people she didn't want to be around. The fact that they were all safely dead already did little to calm her jangled nerves.

Where was Leroy? He'd specifically told her to meet him in the cemetery. She didn't like this, not one bit. Had he lost his mind completely? Was he finally going to kill her this time, burying her in a hole he'd spent the past hour digging? He'd sounded different on the phone, as if he'd been sucking helium. Perhaps he'd gotten stoned out of his gourd and decided to dismiss her permanently.

Sonja walked along the rows, reading names chiselled into the headstones: HERE LIES ALBERT MOSS – A NICE MAN, BUT YOU WOULDN'T TRUST HIM WITH YOUR KIDS... JUDITH MOSS – LOVING WIFE TO ALBERT AND EXTREMELY FORGIVING... MICHAEL CAIN – OVERDOSED ON VIAGRA, HIS WIFE TOOK IT VERY HARD... JEANETTE MACINTOSH – ONE FOOT IN THE GRAVE, THE OTHER STILL MISSING...

Off in the distance, an owl hooted in that ominous way they tend to reserve for cemeteries, haunted houses, and woods utilised by masked maniacs. Sonja was inclined to turn around and run for the road, where the worst she'd have to worry about was the occasional surly punter. She was about to do just that when, somewhere behind her, a shrill cry pierced the night.

"HEE-HEEEE!!!"

That, Sonja thought, *was definitely not an owl*. Whirling around to face whatever it was, she knocked over an old, shoddy gravestone that read: HERE LIES WILLIAM CURDISH – RAPIST, MURDERER, LIAR AND DOWNRIGHT SCOUNDREL. HE WILL BE DEARLY MISSED.

"I-is somebody there?!" she asked, instantly regretting it. Those words had been the last of so many over the years.

"Y'all better believe it, hoe!" a high-pitched voice squealed from the shadows. "Check it!"

It was certainly Leroy, only now he was wearing some sort of garish, red leather jacket. He looked... *lighter*, even in the dark, and his hair... had it always been that greasy, and curly? Perhaps she'd simply never noticed, but Leroy wasn't exactly the kind of pimp-daddy to book himself in for a Jheri curl.

"What's this all about?" Sonja asked, taking a gingerly step back. "I'm losing money being here, which means you're losing money too, which means we're both—"

"It ain't all about the money, bitch," Leroy said softly, almost inaudibly. "You know I like you, don't you?"

Sonja was more than just slightly taken aback. "Never crossed my mind," she replied.

"Well," Leroy continued, "I was wondering if you would be my girl."

"Have you been smoking something?" Sonja asked. "I mean, I'm happy to work for you and all, the way I've been doing, but if you're asking me out—"

"I'm not like other guys," Leroy said, interrupting her.

"You can say that again…"

"No, I mean *different*," he said, glancing up at the full moon (which was odd, seeing as how it had been a waxing crescent not even five minutes ago).

"Look, Leroy, you've obviously got issues, and I—"

That was as far as Sonja got before Leroy dropped to his knees, shaking like a shitting dog. He arched his back as the sound of ripping clothes and cracking bones filled the night. Foam spewed from his mouth, his rapidly growing fingernails clawing at the earth as the tips of his ears tapered to a point.

After a few seconds of what appeared to be absolute agony for the pimp, she finally said:

"You alright?"

Leroy abruptly leapt to his feet. "Yeah, I think so," he said, punching himself in the chest. "Just a bit of indigestion, baby. Now, where the shizznit was I…"

Before Sonja could answer, something latched onto her ankle. She screamed as she leapt back, but the thing grasping her was *strong*, hanging on even as she fell flat on her arse.

"Ah, yes," Leroy said, suddenly remembering where he was. "Tha muthafuckin' zombies…"

Sonja frantically pried the rotten fingers off, snapping phalanges and metacarpals as she staggered to her feet. Another hand punched up from the ground in front of her, and another, then another, and before she knew what was happening, she found herself surrounded by a sea of putrid limbs. Corpses began to pull themselves up from the ground, staggering about, bumping into shit, falling over stuff, and just being generally useless at staying on their feet. Their apparent inability to control their own bodies did little to alleviate Sonja's fears, however. Zombies were zombies, after all, no matter how pathetic they were or how slowly they moved.

"It's close to miiiiiidnight," Leroy sang over Sonja's shoulder, startling her badly. In reaction, she spun around and landed a right hook to his barely recognizable face. The pimp flew backwards like a rag doll, flipping over an effigy resembling Billy Ray Cyrus and landing in an open grave.

Meanwhile, the cemetery had begun to fill with moaning dead people. It was like being at a Donny Osmond concert, only worse. Sonja realised that she was surrounded; zombies were closing in on her from all sides. So, she did what any prostitute worth her salt would have done in a similar situation.

After roughly five minutes of frantic screaming, punctuated by bouts of freaking out and hyperventilation, Sonja had made her peace with God, called the newsagents to cancel her subscription to *People's Friend*, and worked her way through an entire large packet of peanut M&Ms. A few of the zombies might be allergic, after all. She could at least go down with the knowledge that she'd given them a swollen tongue, or a bad case of the shits.

"Ow!" she cried, as the first zombie took a chunk out of her arm. "That came a bit sharp..." The bites that followed were marginally worse than scorpion stings – painful, but not nearly so bad as she'd expected them to be.

Well, she thought, *at least they haven't pulled out my intestines yet.* But no sooner than she'd thunk it, one of the zombies in the dogpile tore into her exposed belly flesh, rummaging around inside as if he'd lost his watch in there.

Bugger, she thought, slipping into the darkness that overtook her.

21

The Pit-Dweller laughed as it drifted over the cemetery, its vocalizations manifest as dark, swirling clouds backlit by the moon.

Zombies! Of all things... You couldn't make this shit up.

Somewhere, George Romero and John Landis would be constructing a strongly worded letter to their respective lawyers, but the thing didn't care about copyright infringement or intellectual property. All it cared about was making the foolish mortals of Bellbrook suffer.

As the zombies slowly filed out of the cemetery, Leroy suddenly leapt from his hole in the ground, did a little graveside shuffle, grabbed his crotch and went "OWWWW!!!"

How very odd, the Pit-Dweller thought to itself, leaving the pimp and his undead horde to their own infernal devices.

22

Meanwhile, an impromptu rap battle was being organized in the middle of Terrence Road. A small stage had been erected with some efficiency, and the performers had already managed to attract quite an impressive crowd. A slow, generic beat thumped from the speakers of a boom box that hadn't been there moments ago.

"Yo, yo, yo," announced the compere, a slight, bespectacled white boy with a complexion that would've made Casper the Friendly Ghost jealous. "We didn't know we'd be doin' this tonight, but since we're all here, let's throw down some beats and kick it olllld schooooooool!"

A cheer went up from the crowd.

"First up, a man who needs no introduction, but for those of you who've never been to one of these before, I'll do one anyway. Best known for his albums, *Ain't No Thing But a Bingo Wing*, and *Shoot Me, Fucker, And I'll Shoot You Back*

(*When You're Not Looking*), I present to you the one, the only, Snoop Diggity!"

The audience went wild as a towering hulk of flesh came bounding up onto the stage, which threatened to collapse beneath the man's weight. He looked less like a man than a creature who eats men and then goes around bragging about it.

"And," the compere continued, "facing him are two newcomers... a couple of right royal gents I've never even heard of before." He shrugged as something like a befuddled snicker fell from his mouth. The audience laughed along with him, though its individual members would be hard pressed to explain why.

"Give it up for the hoarders of ancient shit, a dapper pair of posh poofs – can I say that? Is it still frowned upon? Ahh..." Someone rushed to his side, whispering in his ear that it was indeed considered derogatory, and that they preferred to be called 'nancies' now. "...the tweed-wearing accumulators of antique tat, Roger and Luthor Carter!"

As the twins took the stage, it was to significantly less fanfare, garnering only a small handful of pity claps. No air horns, though.

"He's certainly a big fellow," Roger said, sizing up the twenty-eight stone bulk of Snoop Diggity.

"Just remember what mother used to say," replied Luthor.

Roger thought for a moment. "That's not how you wash it, give it here?"

"No, the other thing she used to say."

"It takes two to tango, but usually one wants to rhumba?"

Luthor sighed. "The bigger they are, the harder they fall."

"She never said *that*, did she?" Roger asked. "If I remember correctly, she said, 'the bigger they are, the harder they'll hit you'!"

"Just goes to show how shit she was," Luthor admitted. "Still, I reckon he'll drop like a sack of potatoes, once we start droppin' science on his bum."

"Yo, yo, yo," Casper the Compere continued. "I want a clean battle. I'd prefer it if you left your mothers out of this, but if you absolutely have to use them, please do so in a respectful manner. Stay on your own side of the stage at all times; we don't want this escalating into a wrestling match. If you *do* cross this invisible line in front of me, you will be disqualified, and ridiculed for the rest of your natural lives. I realise I have a slight speech impediment, but do I make myself clear?"

Snoop Diggity grunted his assent.

"As clear as a Lalique fishbowl," confirmed Roger.

"Okay. Let's hit it!" The compere stepped back, leaving the stage to the identical eccentrics on one side and the menacing man-mountain on the other.

A record scratched and the bass dropped in, then the beat. Anticipating that things might get a little rough despite his warnings, Casper slammed a crash-helmet down onto his head and climbed into a makeshift trench behind the stage.

A riotous mix of estate kids, widowers, dog walkers, vagabonds, and off-duty neurologists, the crowd began to clap along with the rhythm, and soon they began to chant:

"Go Diggity! Go Diggity! Go, go!"

Not one to snub his public, Diggity stepped up, and in a voice that could've crushed rocks, he began:

Snoop Diggity. That's my name and I'll use it,
I'll smash your face if you try to abuse it,
Who the fuck are you two? Jeeves and Wooster?
Do you tickle each other with your little feather dusters?
Which one is which? You the bitch or the butch?
Or do you both miss the feeling of your mother's touch?
With your tweed suits, side partings and glasses,
Just admit it, boys – you're all about asses.
Your daddy should've stopped, took a breath and withdrew.
Instead he left it in, and now there's fuckin' two of you!

The crowd roared in applause. One old lady fist-pumped in the air, screeching, "That's my motherfucking homie, nigga!"

Snoop Diggity abruptly passed the mic to Roger, even though he apparently didn't want it anymore. Luthor whispered words of encouragement, but even he didn't believe that, "kick him in the nuts and we'll make a run for it," would actually help in this situation.

Roger knew they had two ways to go about this: A) share the rap, half and half, or B) utilise the Beastie Boys method, having Luthor join in on the last word of each line. They opted for the latter approach, since it was logistically easier than passing the mic back and forth. It was just like that scene from the end of *8 Mile*, only without the skinny albino fella.

We might be twins, but we like different things,
He likes fatties, and I like thins,
Snoop Diggity, what kind of name is that?
Something Auntie Belle would call a house cat?
And how dare you mock our clothes,
This tweed attracts the hoes,
And while we're at it, bitch, your ass just grows and grows!
You look like Snoop Kong when you mow the lawn,
Baggy swimming trunks looking more like a thong.
What's with the face? There's no need to sulk,

Just 'cos Mommy had sex with The Incredible Hulk.

Convinced they'd won the battle already, Roger dropped the mic, which landed on the stage with a thump and a whine. The twins then performed a secret handshake, which neither one of them had practiced, a series of fumbles and strokes that might've looked a bit odd to anyone but them.

"Phew, that was simply cruuuuuuuuel!" the compere cried, picking up the mic. "You boys might look like a couple of dusty old paedophiles, but you damn sure know your way around a rhyme." He turned to the audience, who were going crazy by this point, jumping up and down, punching each other in the face. A little old lady in the front row lifted up her dress, revealing something rather unsavoury.

"It's down to you, folks. We need a winner. Let me hear it for Snoop Diggity!"

The crowd grumbled and grunted its half-hearted approval. Holding up a sign that read, GO MY LITTLE SNOOPER TROOPER, Snoop's mother screamed so loud, the front window of a nearby Specsavers exploded.

"And what about my tweed-wearing homies, Roger and Luthor Carter?"

The crowd went absolutely bonkers.

"I think we have our winners: the Carter Bros! You guys are the bee's kn..."

He trailed off there, having noticed the gun pointed at him. It wasn't the first time Casper had found himself on the business end of a pistol, but it *was* the first time said pistol fired something more dangerous than water or potato plugs.

The audience fell silent, apart from Snoop's mother, who was now hollering even louder than ever.

"Yo mama didn't raise no fool, boy!"

Roger Carter took a tentative step forward, placing himself between the gun and Casper the Compere.

"What in the name of all that is good and holy do you think you're doing?" Luthor hissed behind his back. "He's going to shoot you in the face!"

"You're not, are you?" Roger said, holding a trembling hand out to Snoop, who was now on the verge of tears. "You wouldn't want to get blood on this Edwardian suit?"

"If he shoots you in the head," Luthor opined, "that suit will be the least of your concerns! Remember what mother used to say?"

"If you don't eat your crusts, your knob will rot off?"

Luthor rolled his eyes. "If it *looks* like a gun, and there's an angry man holding it, then it's best not to get involved!"

"Did she *say* that?"

"Once, I think."

"Look, you couple of poofy old cunts," Snoop sniffed. "I ain't letting you take my motherfucking crown. They don't call me the 'Bellbrook Beatboy' for nothing!"

"Because you keep getting beat..." Roger muttered under his breath.

"I want *him* to tell me I won," Snoop said, jabbing the gun at Casper. "I want *him* to tell all these people that I'm still the best."

"Well, you're the best while you have that gun in your hand," Luthor said, "but, I hate to have to tell you this... these people *saw* what happened. They all know who really won. They saw you get brutally deconstructed through the power of rhyme by a pair of antique dealers in tailored suits."

Snoop thought about this for a moment. If you looked deep into his eyes, you could almost see a team of gangster hamsters running on a wheel.

"Y'all right," he said, then pulled the trigger.

Roger flew backwards from the impact of the slug, his suit and his face utterly ruined.

Turning his gun next upon the audience, Snoop fired indiscriminately into the panicked crowd, but he hadn't counted on someone else packing heat as well. Luthor reached into his freshly-ironed trousers and came out with a French musket that had seen plenty of action in its day, but not much in the two or three centuries since. He managed to load it with powder and ball, and was about to strike flint when a burly construction worker suddenly sidled up to the stage.

"You wouldn't happen to know where I can find a Native American, a GI, or maybe a cowboy or a leather guy, would you?" he asked.

"I *would*, as a matter of fact," Luthor began, taking aim at the raging bull that was Snoop Diggity, "but I'm just a tad busy at the moment."

Pulling the trigger, he soon realised that he would've been better off using the musket as a club. It made a lot of smoke and noise, but as the shot rolled out of the barrel and plunked down onto the stage, he knew that he was royally fucked.

Snoop Diggity charged right into Luthor's frail frame, trampling over and crushing him instantly. The construction worker decided to make a hasty exit before he was wrongly associated with the dead man he'd just been seen speaking with.

As Luthor died, he remembered something his mother used to say:

"When all is said and done, if a fat man's sitting on you, it's best not to struggle."

23

"Looks busy," Clarence said, surveying the line of people queuing outside Knickers. "You think they'll let us jump the line?"

Marcia shook her head. "Not quite, but you see that big lad over there, wearing the doorframe as an overcoat?"

Clarence *did* see him; it was hard not to.

"Well, let me deal with him and we'll get in just fine." She smiled. What she was about to do was unkind, but you didn't get ahead in this game by being nice to people. In fact, most newspapers relegated the agreeable reporters to the basement, where they would spend eternity filing things alphabetically and making sandwiches for the vending machine.

Together they approached the nightclub's entrance. It was at times like this that Clarence wished he had a theme tune, something unforgiving from the 1970s that would start playing whenever things were about to get messy. It just wasn't fair; *The Sweeney* had one, and even those geezers from *Miami Vice*...

"We're from the Bellbrook Observer," Marcia said, stepping toe-to-toe with the larger of the two giants. "It would be really splendid if you could let us in without too much of an ado."

The smaller of the two men – which wasn't saying much – began ogling Marcia like a piece of meat.

"Oooh, Barry, she's a keeper..."

Barry laughed. "Love, I'm going to take your insolence as a gaffe on your part, but only once. If you'd like to join the back of the line, we might let you in around three hours from now, when you get to the door."

Clarence had already begun the long, arduous walk when Marcia went up on her tip-toes, whispering something in Barry's ear as he leaned down to meet her halfway.

"You wouldn't!" Barry gasped. Suddenly he'd gone an incredible shade of crimson.

"I'm afraid I would," Marcia began, "and I'd make sure it was front page, with a *beautiful* picture, which I have on memory-stick back at the office."

Geoff, the other doorman, became intrigued by their discussion. "What's she got on you, Bazza?" he asked, grinning. Clarence couldn't help but notice the massive gaps where his teeth should've been.

"Erm, well, let's just let her in, G. She doesn't look like the type to, er, cause any trouble..." And with that he stepped aside, leaving a massive, Barry-shaped hole in the club's entrance.

"Thank you very much," Marcia said, smiling as she passed through. It was the kind of smile that suggested she was either quite pleased with herself or had just broke wind. "Oh, he's with me," she thought to add, realising the blockade had resumed, leaving Clarence stranded outside.

"He doesn't *look* like he should be with you," Barry replied. "Got a bit of an arsehole look about him, if you ask me."

"Doesn't change the fact he's with me," Marcia said. "Front page, Bazza? Uncensored and in *high* definition."

Once again, Barry stepped aside. "Come on, G, let the man through..."

Clarence walked coolly between the doormen. For a moment, he felt like a slice of soft cheese between two thick wedges of double-hard bastard.

Once they were inside and out of earshot, Clarence pulled Marcia aside. "What exactly did you threaten him with, anyway?"

Marcia leaned in so that he would hear her over the blaring music. "Old Bazza out there is actually Bertha on Tuesdays and Thursdays."

"Aaaah," Clarence replied, "eeeugh..."

If there was one thing he'd learnt in school, it was that it takes all sorts. Unfortunately, those sorts were usually the kind that ended up in jail, institutions, or, apparently, working the door of Knickers Nightclub.

24

"You can't be serious," Ted said, watching his father change clothes. "You can't leave the house looking like that, not while you're monochrome – it'll freak people out!"

Undaunted by his son's criticisms, not-quite-Bill awkwardly pulled on an old pair of striped drainpipes. "Have you *seen* me, son?" he said. "You think I'm just gonna sit around here, waiting until whatever weirdness is happening to me wears off? I look like Elvis Presley, the *King*. It doesn't matter if I'm in black and white. People won't even notice that. They'll be too busy gawping at Elvis feckin' Presley. The lads down at the domino club are gonna be jealous as sin."

"Why, is it their lifelong ambition to be stripped of all colour, too? Look, Dad, I know this is all a bit, well... impossible, but what we need is someone who can figure out what's happening to you, someone who can *help*."

"I don't *need* any bloody help!" not-quite-Bill snapped. "What I need is a little less conversation, and a little more action, please."

"See, that's not *right*," Ted said. "You've been dropping silly Elvis lines for the last half hour. If you go outside, how long will it be before you start looking for the ghetto, or burning houses, stealing cars, stealing liquor from ol' fruit jars?"

"Don't be silly," not-quite-Bill said, standing up. "I wouldn't have a clue how to hotwire a car." He gestured to his clothes. "How do I look?"

"Like something that just fell out of Shakin' Stevens' arsehole," Ted replied. Harsh, yes, but niceties didn't seem to be getting through to his father right about now. "And what about Mum? Huh? While you're off gallivanting as black-and-white Elvis, what do you think she'll be doing? I'll tell you what. She'll be worried sick that you're off looking for a Priscilla to settle down with."

"Your mother knows I would never cheat on her," not-quite-Bill said.

"Yeah, but you're not *you*, Dad," Ted reminded him. If it sounded preposterous, it did because it was. "You're black-and-white Elvis. You look better than most of the geezers in Bellbrook put together. You go walking down High Street like that, you'll have ladies throwing their knickers at you left, right and centre."

"I thought you were trying to convince me *not* to go..." Not-quite-Bill tapped his son playfully on the arm. "Eh? Eh?"

"Dad, now is not the time for..." He trailed off here, lacking the necessary words. "Wait! You're getting... Dad, take a look in the mirror, quick!"

"Don't tell me I'm mutating into Cliff Richard all of a sudden – I couldn't *live* with myself!"

"The mirror, quickly!"

Not-quite-Bill made for the vanity on the other side of the room, cautiously edging around the side of the bed. It was, Ted thought, just how the actual Elvis would have negotiated it, all knee jerks and pelvic thrusts.

His father regarded his reflection with a look of utter confusion upon his face.

"I'm... I've been coloured in!"

"Not just that," Ted said, noticing the change in his father's hair. "Your quiff's gotten bigger, too. If I were to hazard a guess, I'd say you've begun the transformation into late 60s Elvis by this point."

Only that was impossible, wasn't it? In the grand scheme of things, people just don't go from black and white to colour (or black and white in the first place), and they certainly don't age a decade or two in the space of a few minutes.

Not that it bothered not-quite-Bill, who was still turning this way and that before the mirror, as if his biggest concern was whether his pants made his bum look big. "At least I've got some colour back in my cheeks," he said, admiring his bone structure. "These trousers are a bit tighter, though." He popped the top button. "Might need to find something a little less constricting..."

Ted didn't have a clue what to say, other than: *Off you go, then. Don't say I didn't warn you, and be sure to pop into the hospital on the way back from the domino club to get that little Elvis thing checked out...*

Singing and jiving while he swapped his trousers, it was almost as if not-quite-Bill believed what was happening was perfectly normal. "Ah well, bless my soul, what's wrong with me? I'm itching like a man on a fuzzy tree..." He trailed off, laughing. "Funny lyrics, really. I mean, what's a fuzzy tree? Don't know why I wrote 'em like that..."

"Because you didn't," Ted reminded him. "You're not Elvis Presley, Dad. The King is dead, kaput, no more, extinct. Something's happened, something terrible and weird and never in a million years right. You either need a doctor or a priest, and pronto!"

"Wasn't he a Red Indian?" not-quite-Bill said. "I once played a half-breed Indian. *Flaming Star*, that picture was called." He smiled to himself, lost in the fond remembrance. It was all Ted could do not to slap the poor man.

"You weren't in *any* films, Dad. You've never played a Red Indian. You've ordered one from the takeaway, but that's about it."

Not-quite-Bill pulled on a glittery jacket, looking every bit like the host of some inane game-show.

"Look, son, you're obviously jealous of me, and rightly so, but if you could just step aside so I can get my *thang* on, that'd be great."

Am I going to step aside? Ted thought. He'd never stood up to his father before in all his life, and yet it still felt wrong somehow, even though he'd never been more clearly in the right.

"I can't let you leave the house like this," Ted said, trying to make himself look larger by standing up on his tiptoes.

"Then I'm afraid you've left me no choice," not-quite-Bill replied, putting up his dukes. "Did you ever see me in *Kid Galahad*?"

Ted shook his head. "No, but I saw you in your boxers the other day, pissing up the shed."

"I *played* a boxer," his father continued, "Walter Gulick was my name. I was in that one with Charles Bronson!"

"The criminal?" Ted asked, still unsure of what his father had in store for him. "Look, Dad, I don't want to fight you."

"Of course you don't. Nobody *wants* to fight Elvis, but sometimes... Elvis has to fight people. It's the Scots-Irish-German-Cherokee-French-Norman in me." Without warning, he threw a swift jab, coming within an inch of his son's nose.

Realising he'd been left with few options, Ted cocked back and railed not-quite-Bill square in the jaw, sending him flying head over heels. His father landed on the bed, bounced, and came to a rest on its opposite side as an upside-down pair of trousers.

At the evening's onset, all he'd wanted was a nice plate of fish-fingers, some mash, a few episodes of *Heartbeat*, and an early night with his paperback copy of *Fifty Shades of Taupe* (though he usually never read more than a page or two at a time; it was very erotic). Now, both of his parents were unconscious (one of them having been possessed by Elvis), he had an early start in the morning, his head was pounding (a stress migraine, his doctor would call it), and he hadn't seen a single fucking fish-finger all night.

"Talk about a shitstorm..." Ted mumbled, wishing the ground would just open up and swallow him whole before things took another turn (was it even possible?) for the worse.

25

It hovered through the darkness, drifting upon the fish-and-chips flavoured breeze, trying hard not to think about the bastards down below, as they were only making it angrier by the minute.

"Most ancient beings get unearthed by Tony Robinson and the *Time Team*," it fumed, "but not me. I get a bunch of obnoxious Day-Glo Derricks, pissing and cursing and just generally showing no reverence at all. Where's the justice in that?"

Time to take things up a notch, it thought.

Just then, the Pit-Dweller heard... something... far off in the distance. It was awful, like a herd of stampeding bison in a giant steel drum tossed over a cliff, with a pack of howling wolves chasing after it for good measure.

Music, said a voice inside its head.

"If that's music," the Pit-Dweller countered, "then I'm the Earl of Titbottom."

Only it *was* music, or at least what passed for it these godforsaken days. If you listened *really* carefully, stripped away whatever it was making all that shrill racket, and reduced the whole thing to a 4/4 time signature, then you just might catch *something* that could perhaps be considered musical underneath it all, but then of course your eardrums would've imploded by the time you got that far.

Changing course, the Pit-Dweller floated off in the direction of the din, knowing that wherever there was music, there were people, and wherever there were people, there were *souls*.

26

"That's him over there," Lee said, pointing to the VIP area, demarcated by the flimsy rope segregating it from the rest of the club.

"Wait," Alfie said, stumbling as he spilled his drink onto his Crocs. "I thought he was in a chair..."

"H-he *is*," Calvin said. "Th-that's the g-guy from *Sc-Scrubs*. N-next t-to him."

Sure enough, seated beside the guy from *Scrubs* was Professor Stephen Hawking. To Alfie, he didn't look like one of the greatest minds on the planet, but he *was* in the VIP area of Knickers for a reason...

"And just how the hell are we supposed to get to him?" Alfie asked, surveying the security on detail. It looked like the Chicago Bears were having a dress-down day. "I mean, maybe we could just tell your mum he wasn't here, that there was some kind of wheelchair pile-up in the lobby, and he had to be rushed to the hospital."

"Have you *seen* the reporters everywhere?" Lee asked, unconvinced. "He'll be plastered all over tomorrow morning's tabloids, especially if Tara Reid keeps doing *that* to him." He pointed across the room, to where a drunken blonde was writhing in the professor's lap like she needed the money.

"Remind me again," Alfie said, unable to tear his eyes away from the lap dancing woman. "Who is she? She comes across as quite intelligent."

"O-only o-one of the g-greatest actresses of our g-generation," Calvin lied, sounding a bit like the chorus to a well-known song by *The Who*. "G-got one of th-those r-raspy voices, l-like she's b-been deep-throating r-r-razorblades."

"Hawking doesn't seem too interested," Lee remarked. Moments later, the professor shoved Tara Reid off of him using the power of his mind alone.

"I'M A MARRIED MAN. YOU WHORE," he boomed in his robotic voice, cranked up to maximum volume so everyone in the club could hear. "AND F-Y-I. SHARKNADO WOULD NEVER HAPPEN."

Totally unfazed, Tara Reid picked herself up from the champagne-soaked floor, licked her bare arms (*every little bit helps*) and trotted off to the other side of the VIP area, where Michael J. Fox sat twitching in a corner.

"We're *never* going to get in there," Alfie moaned. "You're just gonna have to tell your mum the truth: that we nearly managed to get an autograph, only to find a wall of large, angry-looking men standing between us and the prof."

"Then we'll wait," Lee said, taking a seat. When the chair groaned beneath him, he instantly leapt back up. The short, plump lady presently occupying it had looked like a cushion – an easy mistake. "We'll wait over there, then," Lee said, embarrassed. "He can't stay in there all night, after all. When he comes out, we pounce."

"Pouncing on the disabled," Alfie said, crunching the plastic cup in his hand. "I have to say, even for a gang of thugs like us, that's a new low."

27

Clarence Jameson didn't usually drink (but... *when in Rome)*, which explained why he was sprawled out on the floor at one end of the bar, mumbling nervously about saucer-men from the planet Fzzxthuxx. An individual of dubious sex stood directly over him, failing to notice the pathetic man cowering between his/her fishnets.

"Clarence!" Marcia called. *I turn my back for ten minutes*, she thought, pushing her way through the sea of soused revellers in search of her inebriated photographer.

"Marcia!" Clarence cried, crawling out from underneath the man/woman, "I think the aliens are coming!" Luckily, he/she didn't seem to notice him emerging from behind him/her, as he/she was too busy applying make-up to a face already laden with half a stone of caked-on cosmetics.

"What the hell have you been drinking?" Marcia demanded. Simultaneously stabilising Clarence and keeping the raving lunatic at arm's length was no small feat, yet somehow she managed. "You smell like a urinal cake!"

"I figured it out," Clarence said, slurring his words so much that, for a moment, Marcia thought he was speaking Swahili. "The big bang... it wasn't an earthquake—"

"If I wanted to find out about The Big Bang," Marcia said, "I'd ask the guy in the wheelchair over there."

"No, you daft bint," Clarence chided. "Honestly, you lesbians... no, that big shakeup earlier; it wasn't an earthquake." He leaned in close, as if the information he were about to divulge might place him on the FBI's most wanted list. "It was the *aliens*!"

"Aliens?" Marcia snorted, trying not to laugh. His stupid, drunken face made it nearly impossible to resist.

"S'right," he said, nodding. "What we heard earlier was a *sonic boom*. You see, the alililiens, they would have to break through our atmosphere, wouldn't they?"

Marcia didn't know what was worse, the fact that she was standing in a nightclub with Clarence Jameson, or that what he was saying – in a ridiculously slow and incoherent manner – almost sounded feasible. "Yeah, but wouldn't there have been reports?" she pointed out. "Blurry mobile phone videos, CCTV footage from somebody's dashboard, the usual YouTube crap?"

Clarence looked at her as if she'd just told him the meaning of life. "There's still time for all that," he said. "I'm just looking at the facts. (1) There are no cracks in the ground, which means it was either the lamest earthquake ever or it was really far underground, (2) It didn't sound like a quake. In fact, it sounded more like something letting off from a great altitude, and (3) Do you think they'll let me have another cherry vodka? They're bloody lovely…"

Marcia shook her head. "I need you in tip-top condition," she said, though she doubted that he'd ever been in such a state, even sober. She was just about to say something to that effect when she noticed the camera that had previously been hanging around his neck was no longer there.

"Clarence, where the fuck is your camera?"

Panic washed over him as frantically patted himself down. "Shit! I had it! It was…" He turned, pointed over to the man in the wig and stilettos. And there between her legs – dangling by its strap from his indeterminate genitalia – was the camera.

"Could be worse," Marcia said.

Clarence sighed. "Shit, was I just *under*… her?" He looked like the kind of girl you might take home to mother, if your mother also had a sick sense of humour and a penchant for trannies.

"Go and get your camera back, apologise profusely to the… to *it*, and then get your arse back here. The sooner we get our interview with Hawking, the sooner we can fuck off."

She watched as Clarence made his way through the crowd of revellers, hemmed in on either side by giant speakers blaring some truly god-awful shit. Within her skull, she swore she could almost hear the brain cells dying one by one.

"Well, if it isn't Marcia Martin," came a not-too-friendly voice from behind her. "I didn't think you newspaper broads were allowed out this late. What's the matter? Shit the bed? Scared of a little earthquake?"

Sharon Conker had one of those faces; pretty, but in desperate need of a few well-placed head-butts. "Hey Sharon," Marcia said, feigning warmth as she turned around. "I caught your report earlier; have you seen Marilyn Monroe around? I've *always* wanted to meet her..."

The cameraman behind Sharon began to protest, but instantly ceased when she spun around and gave him the stink eye. "There's no need to film this bit, Clive. I don't think our viewers need to see Miss Martin – it is still Miss, isn't it? Of *course* it is, just look at you..."

Just then, a nearby scuffle distracted the insufferable reporter. "Looks like some guy taking a peek up RuPaul's skirt!" she squealed excitedly. "I hope you're getting this, Clive."

The cameraman shouldered his rig and began to shoot as ordered, but the fight was over just as quickly as it started. Clarence got away with some minor scratches and his camera, while the tranny wilted down onto their barstool after three orgasms and a memory that would last a lifetime.

Don't come over here, not after that, Marcia thought, but it was too late: Clarence was already making his way back towards her. Amazingly, the dense crowd parted for him voluntarily, as if he were liable to go after their crotches as well.

"Got it!" he said to Marcia, wiping the blood from his face.

"Oh my God!" Sharon gasped. "Is that freak with *you*? Jesus, Marcia, I knew things were bad, but I didn't realise you were *this* close to fucking insanity!"

"He works for the paper," Marcia replied, cooly. "And I'm not with him."

"She's a lesbian," Clarence added, "otherwise I'd have been up her like a rat up a drainpipe long ago."

Sharon looked fit to burst, and Marcia wondered just how hard she'd have to hit the bitch to make it happen.

"You're a *lesbian*?" Sharon said. "This just keeps getting better and better! What's the matter? Couldn't find any men to date you, so you switched sides?"

"I didn't realise you were homophobic," Marcia countered. "I'm sure your viewers, not to mention your producers up at the station, would be thrilled to know about that."

"She's *not* homophobic," Clive the cameraman said. To Sharon he added, "Am I supposed to be filming this? I don't have much battery left, and—"

"No, Clive, this is also one of those things you don't really need to film. From now on, only shoot when I say so."

"Will there be a word to let me know when you want me to—"

"*Shoot!*" she said. "The word will be *shoot*." Turning back to Marcia, she continued, "Look, I'm not homophobic, whatever that is, and I really don't care if you're gay, lesbian, queer, or a Scout leader. I just want you to know that we've got things covered here; you might as well go home, back to bed with your man-woman-hermaphrodite, or whatever it is you sleep with, and wait for all this to blow over."

"If it's all the same with you," Marcia said, "we'll stick around. Got an interview with Stephen Hawking; that is, if he's not too pissed to speak to us." She realised how silly that sounded almost immediately; would his robotic voice come out all slurred after sixteen shots of Jagermeister?

"In that case," Sharon said, poking a heavily-manicured talon in Marcia's face, "a piece of advice. Stay out of my way. If I so much as smell whatever shit perfume you're wearing... well, let's just say it won't be pretty." As threats went, it was pretty lame. Marcia didn't know whether to laugh or feel sorry for her.

"Come on, Clive," sneered Sharon. "Some of us have got *work* to do." Abruptly turning away, she spun on her heel so quickly that her hair took a moment to follow suit.

Marcia watched the reporter and her lackey walk off. It was one of those moments when you try to harness dormant telekinetic powers, but when Sharon Conker's head didn't explode, she realised she was wasting her time.

"I think I'm gonna be sick..." Clarence groaned. Marcia turned just in time to catch the contents of her photographer's stomach spewing out onto the dance floor.

28

"So you just suddenly got the urge to dress up as a Native American?" Kavannah asked the stranger. He'd stumbled upon the man climbing out through the smashed front window of *Felicia's Fancy Dress*.

"Weird, huh?" the Native American said. "One minute I was sleeping off a bottle of cheap methylated spirits in the alley behind Marks & Spencer, and the next I was dancing around using a discarded shoe as a tomahawk. I have to admit, at first I thought I'd gone over the edge; like I needed to be sectioned, but then I got to thinking. I thought, maybe I'm *not* mental. Maybe this is just something I need to do in order to take my worthless life back, ya know? That was when I realised I needed the proper get-up; you can't be a

Native American looking like a vagrant with sick down his front."

"So you broke into the fancy dress shop and got yourself an outfit," Kavannah observed. "Of course you did; it would be crazy not to!"

"*Exactly*. And then, once I put it on, I knew I needed to find a cowboy, a GI, a leather man, a construction worker..." he paused, gesturing to Kavannah, "...and *maybe* a motorcycle cop, though I doubt we'll get one of those around here."

"Howdy, fellas!"

Both men turned to face the cowboy who'd suddenly arrived on the scene, sauntering towards them down the alley. He tipped his hat and swiftly drew his plastic, orange-tipped six-shooters, spinning them on his fingers. "Am I late to the party?"

"This is getting just ridiculous!" Kavannah sputtered, though he'd been thinking the same exact thing only moments ago, when he'd helped the lanky Native American safely through the shattered frontage of the dress shop.

"You guys wouldn't happen to know what's going on here, would you?" the cowboy asked, his spurs jingling with each step. "Name's McLoud, by the way, just in case you were thinking I was some random weirdo."

Yeah, because your name changes that...

"Got no idea, mate," the Native American said. "I'm Sid, and this here is Kavannah. We must look like a right bunch of bananas."

They all shared a laugh at this, but quickly fell into an awkward silence. Police sirens could be heard off in the distance.

"I just can't get this *song* out of my head..." McLoud said, removing his hat as if to prove that, yes, he actually did have a head under there. "Do you guys remember that song, about being in the navy? What was it called? The one about being in the navy?"

"Yeah, about being in the navy," Kavannah said. "We *get* it. I think it was called *Sailing*, wasn't it? Rod Stewart?"

"No, that's not it. Great fucking song, though." Mcloud sighed. "Oh well. It'll come to me eventually." He inspected his toy peacemakers in their holsters. "So, what's the plan? We just gonna hang out here until we figure out what's going on, or..."

"I think we need to keep moving," Sid suggested, watching one of the feathers from his headdress float down to the pavement. "I've got this weird feeling. Like I need to dance, but can't, not until we find the rest of our posse. Odd, huh?"

"*Very,*" Kavannah agreed. "Okay, then. No point hanging around this alley like a trio of kerb-crawling psychopaths. Let's roll out!"

"Hey, that's *my* line," McLoud said. "Let's hit the trail, find ourselves some serving wenches, and a bottle of something milky!"

"Did cowboys *say* that?" asked Kavannah.

"Not sure," McLoud replied, "but if they did, I'll bet they were a bunch of dicks."

29

When not-quite-Bill opened his eyes to find himself strapped to a chair in the kitchen, he didn't look one bit amused. Standing beside the table were both Edith and Ted. His wife looked frightened; his son looked determined. Both of them, not-quite-Bill thought, could go straight to hell.

"Oh, so *this* is how we're going about it, eh?" he said. "Tying me up. Well, let me tell you, ain't no ropes ever woven strong enough to hold Elvis." He struggled ineffectually for a moment before settling back down, panting like an overheated cocker-spaniel. "All right. Please, just let me go. I promise I won't try jiving none. I don't even feel like dancing anymore, *or* singing. This whole thing is just plain silly..."

"Dad, we've got the doctor on his way," Ted said. "Should be her any minute." He'd called Dr. Cain half an hour earlier, while not-quite-Bill was still knocked out on the bedroom floor.

"Hang on a minute," not-quite-Bill said. "You've called *Lucius*? You called him and told him to come over because I've turned into Elvis Presley and you don't know what to do with me?"

That, Ted thought, was about the gist of it, though he'd left out the bit about Elvis, as he hadn't wanted to sound like a *complete* nutter on the phone.

"Well this is just spiffing," not-quite-Bill grunted, still wriggling against his bonds. "And what about you, Edith? You can't say you don't prefer me like this. I'm a hunk-a-hunk-a-burning love, for Christ's sake!"

"I want my husband back," Edith said, pouring herself a large glass of something strong. "If I'd wanted to marry Elvis Presley, then I would have gone with Bobby Graceland when I had the chance."

Not-quite-Bill rolled his eyes. "Bobby Graceland was a two-bit tribute act from Tipperton. And do you *always* have to bring him up every time something remotely bad happens to us? *Sheesh*, I never bring up Elsie-May Tanner, do I?"

Edith almost choked on her moonshine. "You just did!" she said. "I can't believe, after all these years, you're still thinking about what might've been with that little slu—"

"This is not happening..." Ted said, pinching his nose between thumb and forefinger. His head was pounding; his ears were aching, and his stomach was rumbling from the lack of fish-finger tea. "Now look. The doctor will be here any minute. When he comes, I want you *both* to be on your best behaviour."

Edith nursed her glass, tried her best not to break down, and thought about Bobby Graceland. *Is it too late? I've still got his number, and there are a few years left in this old body yet...*

After five minutes of unbearable silence – broken only by not-quite-Bill, occasionally humming a few bars from 'Suspicious Minds' – there came a sharp knock at the door. Ted jumped up from his seat at the table and went to answer it. *Please, please, PLEASE tell me you can fix my broken dad.*

Immediately upon opening the door, Ted realised that Doctor Cain was in no fit state to perform any miracles tonight. His silver hair –what remained of it – was spiked straight up at the moon, sharp and severe, and something had been stuck through his nose. Upon closer inspection, Ted saw that it was a safety pin. Blood had dried upon the doctor's cheek and chin, and he was wearing what appeared to be a grimy denim jacket, but the myriad chains, studs, and patches covering it made the exact material hard to tell.

"What's the fucking matter?" Doctor Cain asked. "Ain't you ever seen a punk before, boy?"

Now, Doctor Cain was a devout Catholic, the kind of man who'd sit your kitten while you went off to Ibiza for some much-needed sex, sea, and sun. His CD collection was comprised mainly of hymns and choir music. If anything, Dr. Lucius Cain was the last person you'd expect to show up at your door sporting a homemade piercing and a Mohican that would've made Sid Vicious jealous.

"Well, let me fucking in, you daft prick," the doctor said. "I can't help your dear ol' daddy standing out here like a tit in the breeze, can I?"

Ted was about to say that he supposed so, that he was sorry for being so rude, when suddenly he noticed a cowboy, a Native American, and a construction worker ambling down the street together. *Now there's something you don't see every day*, he thought, but then today had hardly been what anyone would call 'everyday'. He had Elvis Presley tied to a chair in his kitchen, and now Johnny Rotten PhD was standing on his doorstep.

"You'd better come in," Ted said, stepping aside. "He's through there. Be careful, though. I don't think he's going to be very nice to you."

Striding into the kitchen, Dr. Cain harrumphed dismissively, as if he were looking at nothing more than a nasty rash or a particularly weak case of Man Flu. "I see what you fucking mean," he said, giving not-quite-Bill the once-over. "You know who he looks like? He looks like Elvis Fucking Presley."

"That's what I meant to tell you," Ted said. "I didn't want to say anything on the phone, because, well, you know... anyway, he didn't look like this at tea-time. You know what Dad looks like normally."

The doctor nodded. "A heart attack waiting to happen," he said. "I knew your father when he had his first piles, and he was fucked even then."

Not-quite-Bill became flabbergasted. "I'm in the room, ya know," he sputtered. "Show a little tact, will you?"

"He even sounds like fucking Elvis," Dr. Cain laughed. "Repeat after me," he said to not-quite-Bill, "*Well...*"

Confused, yet hesitant to refuse the doctor's order, not-quite-Bill complied.

"Well..."

"*It's one...*"

"It's one..."

"*For the money...*"

"Look, this is silly!" not-quite-Bill snapped. "And what the hell have you come as, Lucius? You look like you've been dragged through the 70s backwards."

"What is it with you freaks?" Dr. Cain sneered. "It's like the punk movement never happened in Bellbrook. Ain't cha ever heard of *Stiff Little Fingers? Black Flag?* The fucking *Ramones?*"

"Doctor, I hate to say it, but you wouldn't have heard of them before tonight, either." Ted didn't want to be the one, but someone had to call him out. "You're not a punk. You've never been a punk, even when it was popular – which, in Bellbrook, was never – *and* you've basically punctured your face for reasons unknown, your hair looks daft, and... I mean, what have you got in it, even?"

"I couldn't find any gel," Dr. Cain replied, "so I went with the next best thing."

"Which was?" asked Ted, genuinely intrigued.

"I had a fried egg for breakfast this morning," the doctor said. "I hadn't washed up yet, so I used the fat from the pan."

"See!" Ted cried. "That is not normal behaviour for a doctor. In fact, the men in white coats have a place for people like you, and for my father, who suddenly looks and sounds exactly like a man who's been dead for nearly forty years."

The doctor thought for a moment. It was an extremely surreal moment for Ted, his gaze drifting over a punk who wasn't a punk, but an old guy with a safety pin in his face and fat in his hair; his mother, still terrified, trembling and doing her very best not to pass out again; and the man tied to the chair – not-quite-Bill – whose testicles had once harboured the seed of his existence.

"Nah, that's bollocks," Dr. Cain finally said. "I *am* a punk!" As if to prove his devotion to all things anarchic, he leaned across to the countertop and knocked an empty glass down onto the lino, where it shattered. "See?"

Ted was, for want of a better word, resigned. "Okay, if you say so... Look, Doc, I don't know what's going on around here, but I really think we need to get my dad to the hospital. Maybe they can—"

But the doctor wasn't listening; he was looking around the kitchen for something. "You don't have any alcohol going, do you?" he asked. "I swear I'm drier than Ghandi's fucking flip-flop."

"I don't think he's going to help us," Edith muttered, low enough so only Ted could hear. He nodded in response; his mother had a knack for stating the bleeding obvious.

"Okay, Doc, thanks for coming," Ted said, ushering him towards the door. "I'm sure you're *very* busy. We'll take care of things here!"

"When I was on tour with The Clash," the doctor said, "I once caught the clap so bad that I had to perform surgery on my own—"

"Like I said, Doc, thanks for coming." Ted manhandled the maniac back down the front hall, before his nose could drip anymore blood onto the floor. "I'll be sure to recommend you to *nobody*, and will be writing a strongly worded letter to the Head of General Practitioners regarding this incident."

"You *do* that," the doctor spat in response. "You fucking *do* that! I ain't a doctor no more. ANARCHY!!!" Thrust out into the night, he promptly took off down the street, overturning rubbish bins and kicking stray cats along the way.

Ted quickly locked the door behind him, falling against it and taking a deep breath.

"Oh, what are we going to do?" Edith sobbed. She'd crept up beside Ted like a ninja; a geriatric ninja wearing a flowery muumuu.

"I... I don't know just yet," Ted replied, pulling his mother in for a hug, which was weird as he couldn't remember the last time he'd done so, and had forgotten how musty she smelled. "But if we don't do *something* soon, I think you'll be back on the market, and I'll be learning to fish on my own."

And that, Ted thought, as his mother broke down completely, *is NOT the way to console the woman responsible for fish-fingers...*

30

Meanwhile, the Pit-Dweller had begun to consolidate in the sky above Knickers Nightclub, just before midnight.

Ooh, the witching hour, it thought, wincing at the sheer campness of the voice in its head. It decided to do as little thinking as possible from that point on; the poor thing was already sexually confused enough as it was, lacking a penis, vagina, or any other tangible bits to speak of.

On its way over, it had transformed three men into the Bee Gees, and a deranged blonde woman was now running the streets with gaudy cones for tits. It made about as much sense to the Pit-Dweller is it did to those affected, but whatever was happening to the wretched residents of Bellbrook, it seemed to be doing the trick. The Pit-Dweller knew that, by the end of the night, easily half of the townsfolk would be dead. Those left living would be driven insane, and those attempting escape would explode in a great conflagration of shitty B-sides and one-hit wonders on the outskirts of town.

The thing looked down upon the people far below, intent upon destroying each and every one of them before sun-up. It felt good to be back; it owed them that much. *This must be how The Spice Girls felt*, it thought, *when they stopped making dodgy perfume and decided to reform...*

"The *who*?" the Pit-Dweller said, still just as confused as ever by all the peculiar shit rattling around in its mind. It knew, for some reason, all about Baby Spice, Ginger Spice, Mel B and C, and one that it couldn't quite put its finger on, although it knew she was famous for something... It also knew that Chris Rea's husky voice was due to a sword-swallowing accident back in 1969, and that every time Cliff Richard releases a Christmas album, a child in Mozambique dies of dysentery.

How did it know these things? *Who ARE these freaks?* it thought, unable to resist its own curiosity. *Alas, no time to dilly-dally.* There were people in that building down there, people for it to devour, one way or t'other.

Swooping low, it drifted between the pair of burly idiots guarding the door, slowly seeping inside. The pungent stench within was far worse than anything the Pit-Dweller had ever been exposed to in its centuries underground: a nauseating effluvium of beer, vomit, body-odour, and cheap *eau-de-toilette* (with the emphasis on toilet).

Further it invaded, slathering patrons with its unseen ectoplasm, licking their bums and faces with its imperceptible tongue. By the time it hit the dance floor, it could have done with a nice cup of tea and a lie-down.

"No rest for the wicked," it said, soaring up to the house lights, which seemed confused as to which colour they ought to be.

So many people, so many souls, and so many... terrible fashion choices...

31

"And now, ladies and gentlemen of Knickers Nightclub," the DJ announced, "can the owner of the white Vauxhall Astra, registration DB2 4XY, kindly shift it before we have no choice but to set it afire?" He paused before continuing, "We have a very special treat for you tonight. If you'll turn your attention to the stage, you will notice some guitars, a drum-kit, and one of those singing stick-things up there. Now, if you know your music – and I sure do – then you *know* this can mean only one thing..."

A half-hearted cheer went up from the crowd.

"That's right, people. Put your hands together for our very special guest, Mrs. Marilyn... what? Oh, it's a *boy*... I've just been told that Marilyn is, in fact, a boy, so please put your hands together for... it's a bit of a daft name for a boy, though, isn't it? I mean... what? Brian? So why doesn't he just use... ladies and gentleman, would you please welcome to the stage, the boy with a girl's name, Mr. Marilyn Manson!"

The crowd applauded. In the VIP area, Stephen Hawking cried "BRAVO" in his monotone, robotic voice, and that guy from *Scrubs* put Tara Reid down long enough to fist-pump the air. Unfortunately, Michael J. Fox had had to leave early, as his parents forbade him from staying out after midnight, a little like one of those evil green critters you should never urinate on.

The lights went down as Marilyn took to the stage, his band of misfits following just behind. They each took their places by their respective instruments, and Marilyn, of course, took the mic.

"Knickers Nightclub!" he roared. It was, the DJ thought, definitely a boy. So confusing. "Are you ready to raaaaawwk!?"

Everyone in the audience made devil-horns with their fingers; either that or a flash-mob had suddenly formed upon the dance floor, intent on teaching everyone how to count to two.

From up in the rafters, the Pit-Dweller watched, silently pondering what had gone wrong with the world, and trying desperately to figure out the pasty-faced fuckers on stage, who were obviously trying to steal its thunder.

"Boys and Ghouls, creatures of the night, you demonic little shits that crawled out of my anus when I wasn't looking." He was charming, this Marilyn. "We're going to do something a little bit different tonight. Who here knows 'The Wheels on the Bus'?"

The club-goers murmured amongst themselves, looking at each other in confusion. Gradually, they began to raise their hands, until everyone but the most stone-faced in attendance admitted to remembering the nursery rhyme.

"Good, good, because we wanted to show you lovely little minions of darkness that we're not just a metal band with songs about how the drugs love us, and the beautiful people. Tonight, we'll be playing a selection of classic children's songs – with our own distinct flavour, of course – starting with *this* little ditty."

Marilyn counted the band in, and suddenly they launched right into a shrieking, distorted rendition of 'Humpty Dumpty'. After a few moments of utter bewilderment, the audience got right behind them. A mosh-pit – not too violent, due to the whimsical nature of the song – formed in the centre of the dance floor. It was during the more up-tempo 'Incy Wincy Spider' that one man had to be stretchered out, and several others were ordered – by doormen dressed as The Blues Brothers – to "Calm down before you have someone's eye out!"

32

"Now's our chance!" Lee said, spotting Professor Hawking at the bar, alone. Someone had attached one of those helmets – a curly straw and space for four cans – to his bonce. "If we're quick about it, we can reach him before his minders even notice."

Alfie shrugged. If they got kicked out of the club, it wouldn't necessarily be a bad thing as far as he was concerned. He preferred his music with no guitars, and definitely no baa baa-ing black sheep. "Come on, then. Let's get this over with…"

"H-have you a-asked yourself why H-Hawking is at the b-bar on his o-own?" Calvin asked, sidestepping a woman who could have moonlighted as a Russian shot-putter when she wasn't chugging from a keg.

"He probably just wants a break from this lot," Lee offered. "I mean, every day he has people telling him what to do, where to go, when to poop, when not to poop. This is like a vacation for him."

"A vacation at the bar of Knickers Nightclub?" Alfie said. "Cancel my fortnight in Barbados, there's a stool with my name on it."

"Look," Lee said, "once we get his autograph, we can leave." He was now standing within just a few feet of the professor's minders, and for the first time that night he became flummoxed. "What should I *say* to him?"

Alfie groaned, and Calvin was just C-Ca-Calvin.

"You need to ask about life, the universe, and everything in it; question him on the formation of black holes and the continuing expansion of the universe, and then, you know, once you've built the foundations for a lifelong friendship with a man possessed of an IQ higher than your top score in Tomb Raider, see if he'll sign your little black book for you?"

"Is all that necessary? I mean, I just want his sig—"

"Just ask for his fucking autograph so we can get the hell out of here!"

"Alright, I'm going in..."

Lee made his move for the bar, where Professor Hawking had lined up a neat little row of colourful, luminous shots for himself. *But how is he going to do them on his own?* Lee wondered, considering the man's paralysing neurodegenerative disease.

Hawking's minders were so entranced by Manson's screaming rendition of 'Ten Green Bottles', they didn't even notice Lee slip by.

"Professor Hawking. Do you mind if I call you Professor, or do you prefer Mister? Or *Steve?*"

Professor Hawking glanced over at him with something like distaste, although it wasn't all that easy to guess what he was thinking from his eyes alone.

"I'M GETTING ABSOLUTELY BLASTED," he replied. "ALONE. IF YOU DON'T MIND." There was something about his staccato, automaton voice that made the dismissal even more potent; it was like being reproached by a Dalek, or severely reprimanded by R2D2.

Unperturbed, Lee continued, "Yeah, I can see that, Steve. The thing is, my Mum's a *huge* fan of yours. She's seen everything you've ever done, and read all your books as well. I hate to say it, but I've watched her face when you're on the telly, and she's licking her lips and pouting the whole time. I don't suppose you'd want her phone num—"

"I WANT TO BE LEFT ALONE," Hawking interrupted.

Lee was getting a bit perturbed himself by this point, but there were laws against slapping disabled people with autograph books, so he held it out gently instead. "Can I just ask a quick favour, Steve. It would mean the world to my dear old mother if you could put your scribble – or just a bit of spit – on this here page."

Hawking's voice modulator almost seemed to sigh. "CAN'T A GUY GET BLADDERED IN PEACE ANYMORE."

Lee held the book just below the professor's chin, waiting for some sign of salivation. "Just a spec of drool, please? Don't want it smearing Professor Brian Cox's entry, or worse, Brian Blessed's..."

And then – just as Hawking was about to give up the goods, as Marcia and Clarence were about to approach him for an interview, as Sharon Conker and her cameraman were about to tackle them first, and as that guy from *Scrubs* was leading a thoroughly inebriated Tara Reid into the toilets – something incredibly odd happened.

Marilyn Manson and his band abruptly stopped playing; the revellers, who'd been enjoying a much heavier version of 'Old King Cole' only moments ago, had ceased dancing and were now trying to fathom just who the man moonwalking onto the stage thought he was.

"It's Jacko!" one man shouted. "Jacko's back! Lock up your daughters!"

"And sons!" said another.

"And chimps!"

Marilyn Manson regarded the interloper with bemused derision. Into the microphone, he sniggered and said, "Well, well, well; we've got a joker joining us on stage tonight. What's your name, freak?"

The strange man moonwalked all the way across the stage before spinning around and snatching the mic right out of

Marilyn's skinny, pale hands. The crowd began to boo and hiss, as if this were all part of some twisted Christmas pantomime. From the safety of his booth, the DJ cried, "He's behind you!" but nobody laughed. Such was the life of a DJ.

"Y'all havin' a good time?" the party-pooper asked in an effeminate voice, holding out the microphone for the crowd to respond. Unfortunately, they didn't quite grasp the concept. "Heee-hee!" the man suddenly squealed, popping up onto his toes and grabbing his crotch.

"Shit, that's my *pimp*," one woman whispered into her husband's ear. It wasn't the kind of thing he'd expected to hear, and at first he thought his missus was joking, but when she thought to add, "He'll fucking *kill* me if he sees me here! Honey, we have to leave. Leroy's a vicious bastard. There's no telling *what* he might do to the kids," a feeling in the pit of his stomach told him she was telling the truth. As the soon-to-be-divorced couple headed for the exits, the man on stage continued:

"Y'all dancing the motherfucking night away, huh? Us too, us too. In fact... Shamone... Shamone... Shamone..." He performed a few spastic moves until his shoulder popped out of its socket, leaving his arm dangling listlessly at his side. "I brought a few friends to meet y'all!"

A chorus of guttural moans erupted from backstage, prompting Marilyn Manson to leap into the arms of his bassist, who gently stroked his head.

"I brought my motherfucking *Thriller* zombies!"

Right on queue, hundreds of snarling, groaning dead people tore through the curtains, spilling out across the stage and down onto the dance floor. Women screamed, men screamed, and the Russian shot-putter grunted in dismay. People stampeded for the exits, but the shit thing about Knickers was its single-file policy; an orderly queue had to be formed first, providing a convenient buffet line for the ravenous undead monstrosities.

Whenever a zombie took down one the panicked patrons, ripping their flesh to shreds, it did a little dance or a body-pop. One of them was spinning on its head in the middle of the now thoroughly vacated dance floor. With the sheer amount of blood and guts that had already been slicked across it, the advanced breakdancing move was actually quite easy to pull off.

The only trouble was stopping. When the zombie's whirling legs finally reached a high enough velocity to lift it airborne, it wished it had stuck with simple splits and leg-kicks, like its mates down below, as it flew off across the club.

Meanwhile, by the toilets, that guy from *Scrubs* and Tara Reid were desperately fighting off the encroaching ghouls.

Where's Michael J. Fox when you need him? that guy from *Scrubs* thought as a zombie lunged at him, all claws and teeth. It was like being savaged by Janet Street-Porter.

"No, that guy from *Scrubs*!" Tara Reid screamed. She'd worked with him on several episodes of the hospital-based comedy, and even *she* couldn't remember his name. Several zombies overpowered her as she dove for the bag of coke in his pocket, dragging her down onto the floor with them. Eagerly devouring her flesh, they abruptly lost their appetites after hitting her breast implants, scraping their rotten tongues off and picking shreds of silicone from their teeth. It was like discovering your grandma had forgotten to take the giblets out of the Christmas turkey.

Up onstage, Marilyn Manson's bandmates were fending off the creatures with their respective instruments, swinging guitars, keyboards and mic stands at the advancing horde. The drummer had taken to using his symbols as makeshift shields, deflecting choreographed claw attacks. As for Marilyn himself, he'd dug his long, black nails into the backstage curtains, scaling them like a terrified cat as he screamed at the top of his lungs.

"Are you getting all this!" Sharon Conker said, dodging one zombie and kicking another in the lady-parts.

"You didn't say shoot!" Clive the Cameraman protested. "You specifically said—"

"I know what I said, you remedial buffoon, but surely you can see that *this* is newsworthy!"

Clive stopped to take in the carnage all around them; it was like something out of a really bad horror film, one of those Italian jobs with Play-Doh special effects and subtitles that made about as much sense as a drunken David Hasselhoff. "So do you *want* me to film or not?" he asked, still a bit uncertain. "I—"

Just then, a decapitated head flew across the room, knocking the camera from his hands and smashing it on the floor.

"Well, that's fucked," Sharon said, kicking the chunks of busted plastic and circuitry that could have been her ticket to winning Newscaster of the Year. She'd always wanted one of those little trophies on her mantel, the one with the busty lady holding a microphone, and now, she would never get one. "We need to get out of here!" she screamed, starting to panic. "Over there!" She pointed to a side door near the stage, which several other club-goers were already escaping through.

Suddenly, though, Sharon couldn't move. She felt... *violated*, somehow, as if the entire world had suddenly started talking about her behind her back, saying nasty things about her hair, her make-up, her haemorrhoids...

"You okay?" Clive asked. "Come on, we've got to go!"

She just stood there, blank, all the colour drained from her face. If Clive had been a gambling man, he would have put his house, its contents, and his Ford Tranny Van on Sharon upchucking within the next ten seconds. Luckily for him, though, all the other patrons were too busy getting killed at the moment to take his bet, because she abruptly snapped out of it in roughly half that time. "Come on then, what are we waiting for!?" she yelled at him, grabbling his arm as she ran for the door.

With Clive loping along beside her, she had the strangest feeling that something terrible, and hopelessly irreversible, had just happened to her. If she could have seen the moustache forming on her upper lip, like a freakish black caterpillar, she would have lost her shit completely.

33

"What the *hell* is going on!?" Marcia screamed, cowering behind the bar with Stephen Hawking and several strangers. "Oh, Professor, what *are* those things?! And why has Michael Jackson risen from the dead?!"

Hawking did everything in his power to tell the crazed woman he had no idea, but, having been relieved of his chair and its built-in voice unit by some opportunistic hooligans shortly after the rioting began, he was literally left speechless.

"Well, this is awkward," Marcia said, scanning the petrified faces of those around her. "Does *anyone* know what's going on out there?"

"Shombiesh," one rather sloshed teenager suggested. "Lotsha shombiesh…"

"Thanks for that," said Marcia. "Anyone else?" She felt like that strict History teacher, the one who would put you in the stationary cupboard if you couldn't tell them the name of every Tudor since records began.

"Like I said earlier," came a voice from behind her. "It's the *aliens.*"

"Oh, Clarence, how long have you been there?" It was a serious question; she hadn't noticed him a moment ago.

"I was the one who dragged you behind the bar," he said, astounded by Marcia's sudden amnesia. "Anyway, it's *got* to be aliens. I always knew they'd taken Jackson, back in the eighties. It was all a bit… *convenient*, wasn't it? I mean, one minute he was fine, and next…"

"That man out there is not the *real* Michael Jackson," Marcia said. "For one, he's black."

"Yeah, I thought that was a bit strange," Clarence admitted, "but I put it down to the lighting."

"Did you see what happened to Manson?" said a girl wearing more kohl than Robert Smith on a night out. Her tears had left long black streaks down her face; Marcia didn't know whether to comfort the poor thing or give her tips on proper eyeliner application.

"Tha shombiesh got 'im," said the drunken boy. "He wash almosht to tha rafters when he shlipped."

"It's what he would have wanted," said the gothic girl, crossing herself over her ample exposed cleavage.

Marcia rolled her eyes. "We need to get the hell out of here," she said. "Did anybody see where the professor's chair went?"

"Last I saw it, some zombies were using it as a dance prop," Clarence said. "To be honest, the choreography was a bit jerky, and one of them was missing a leg, which, for me, basically ruined the whole routine."

"Ish tha door clear yet?" Drunk Boy asked.

Marcia climbed up onto her haunches, took a deep breath, and snuck a quick peek over the top of the bar.

The place had cleared out quite a bit by that point, but the club was still thick with freestyle-dancing freaks, cleaning up the remains of those unfortunate fatties who'd been too slow to escape. Up onstage, a zombie was eyeing up Marilyn Manson's corpse, but quickly lost interest after realising there was more meat on a chicken wing. The rest of the band had been completely torn apart, their broken and blood-spattered instruments left strewn across the stage. Apart from the Blues Brothers lookalikes, still holding their own against the zombies out on the dance floor, there wasn't another living soul in sight.

Marcia slowly lowered herself back down behind the bar, where she was met by a wall of expectant faces.

"What's it look like out there?" Goth Girl asked.

"Not good," Marcia said, "but the doors are clear at least. We should be able to make a run for it!"

"What about the professor?" Clarence asked. "I mean, without being politically incorrect, I just don't think he'll be able to keep up."

Shit. She'd forgotten about Hawking. As she stared into his sad, defeated eyes, she saw something, a flicker, but nothing more. *Go on without me*, they said. *I'll only get you all killed.* At least, that's what she hoped he was trying to communicate; in truth, he was saying, *You'd better not fucking leave me here with a roomful of dancing zombies! Don't you know who I am? The human race is screwed without me... I wasn't going to say anything, but I've perfected time travel. I have the blueprints stashed away in my knicker drawer at home. It's all there, all except for one vital piece, which is still in my head.*

"He wants us to go on without him," Marcia said, reaching down to squeeze his immobile hand.

No! You fools! Don't you—

"Right, come on then you lot," Marcia said to Goth Girl, Drunk Boy, and Clarence. "Let's get out of here before the professor changes his mind."

Fine, go then, see if I care... no, please, I didn't mean that... you absolute selfish wankers...

"Run straight for the door. Any zombies get in your way, don't even think about dancing with them; it's all just a ploy to get close enough to bite you. Don't stop running until we're clear of the building, and Clarence..."

"What?"

"Get as many photos as you can on the way out. This is going to be front-page news tomorrow, if we live that long."

34

Watching the chaos unfold, the Pit-Dweller couldn't help feeling a bit awkward despite itself. There was something so *sordid* about it, but try as it may to look away, there was simply no use.

And to think I wasn't gonna come out tonight, it thought, sounding more like John Inman than ever before. The zombies had been a fluke, but the Pit-Dweller was still just as proud of them as a Birmingham mother on her son's first court date.

When three young men suddenly bolted from the toilets in a mad dash for the door, it wasn't about to let them go that easily.

"I don't think so, you little bastards," the Pit-Dweller said, swooping down like an eagle after dormice.

They were soon joined by four others; two men and two women. Having jumped the bar on the other side of the room, they'd apparently picked the same exact moment to hightail it out of there.

Just before they reached the exit, the Pit-Dweller enveloped the lot of them in its ancient evil miasma, cackling like Vincent Price as it overtook the group of desperate stranglers. If they noticed its presence, they didn't give anything away, but as they went crashing through the door and out into the street, the Pit-Dweller knew they wouldn't get far. It wouldn't be long before it brought them and everyone else in this godforsaken town to their knees.

35

"You can't keep me tied up like this," protested not-quite-Bill. "This isn't Guantanamo, and I'm not some Jihadi twat-bucket from Durki-Durkiland! I'm your father, and I demand you loosen these ropes right now, or I'll ground you for the rest of your natural life."

Ted sighed. "I'm pushing fifty, Dad," he said. "Your grounding days are over."

"Perhaps we *should* untie him," Edith said, gradually putting the final pieces of a jigsaw puzzle (the difficult one with the baked beans on it) into place.

"Finally," not-quite-Bill said. "Sense at last!"

Ted had known his mother would crack; she'd always been the forgiving type, like when the newspapers had gotten caught recording private phone conversations. "Look at it this way," she'd said. "If Hugh Grant had been up to his usual terrorism, people wouldn't be so quick to complain." Or when Harold Shipman was found guilty of fifteen murders, with another two-hundred-and-thirty-five ascribed to him, she'd said, "To be fair, his victims *were* getting on a bit. If you think about how much they would have ended up costing the NHS, it's hardly surprising that a doctor took the time and effort to do something about it."

Yes, Edith Butcher was an exceptionally forgiving person, but Ted had never believed her to be *completely* off her rocker. "We can't untie him, Mum," Ted said. "Look at him. He's swelling before our very eyes..."

"Exactly," she said, still studying the baked beans puzzle on the table before her. "If we don't untie him soon, those ropes will cut off the circulation to his arms and legs. He'll just be a blobby stump in a chair, and I don't want that, not in my kitchen."

"Look, I promise I won't try nothing, uh-huh," he said, repressing the residual quiver in his upper lip. "I don't fancy going out anymore; those days are behind me. All I want is some food and a nice lie down. This has been a very stressful night for me. To say I'm all shook up would be an understatement."

Ted was torn. On one hand, he knew it wasn't right to keep his father bound like this; on the other, the man in the chair wasn't truly his father anymore, just some bloated guy in a gaudy, glittering outfit. If there *was* some way to get his old man back, he doubted they'd be able to figure things out and implement it before...

"Quick!" not-quite-Bill suddenly blurted out. He looked positively terrified. "Something's happening. Untie me before..." He groaned and began to shudder violently, sliding backwards in his chair.

Edith abruptly quit her puzzle and launched into full-bore panic. "Oh, Ted, quick! Do something before he has a heart attack!"

Ted raced over and began briskly untying the ropes, wishing he hadn't done them so tight in the first place. "It's okay, Dad," he said. "I'm setting you free! Everything's gonna be alright..."

Still seated in his chair, not-quite-Bill continued to write and moan. Ted didn't want to think about it, but the sounds and smells now emanating from his father's trousers suggested he'd be needing a good cleaning up after this. The scuff-marks on his blue suede shoes would be the least of not-quite-Bill's worries when his arse was completely covered in shit. *Clean up your own backyard*, Ted couldn't help thinking, which only seemed appropriate to their situation.

No sooner had Ted undone the final knot when his father lurched violently forward, landing face-first with a meaty slap on the linoleum. Ted moved the chair out the way and turned the man over, trying in vain to avoid inhaling his pungent stench.

"Is he dead?" Edith asked. "Oh my God, is he breathing?"

"He's breathing," Ted said, watching his father's chest rise and fall. "I think he's just passed out from the... sudden weight gain."

And it *had* been quite sudden indeed. Not-quite-Bill's sparkly jacket only had one button left on it; the rest of them had popped off and whizzed across the kitchen like little plastic bullets as he'd ballooned up. The man was so packed into his trousers now, it was remarkable to think that they'd *ever* fit him.

"We need to get him out of these clothes," Ted said, wincing at the thought.

"I was thinking that back when he was still late 60s Elvis," Edith said.

"Get his boots off," Ted said, grabbing not-quite-Bill under the arms. "He's turning into Fried Banana Elvis. Fuck knows what's going to happen to him next."

With his boots, trousers and jacket finally removed (they'd ultimately had to cut his clothes off), all that remained was a bloated old man with an Elvis quiff, sprawled out upon the shit-smeared lino. Ted hadn't seen anything so sad and pathetic since Tom Cruise decided to use Oprah's sofa as a trampoline.

"What's... uhhh... what happened?" not-quite-Bill muttered, coming to. It must have been quite confusing for him; after all, a minute ago he'd been late 60s Elvis.

"Dad, just lie still," Ted said, looking away in disgust. It was all he could do to keep the vomit down. For the first time that night, he was glad his mother had forgotten the fish-fingers, as they most certainly would have made an encore appearance by now. "We're going to get you to the hospital."

A panicked expression formed upon not-quite Bill's newly distended face. "I hope you're at least going to dress me first," he said, crinkling his nose. "Has someone farted?"

"Let's get him into the bathroom," Edith said. "I can finish my jigsaw later."

Once they'd cleaned him up, they sat him on the toilet and discussed their options, which were: (1) hope this whole thing were just some mass-delusion, and that everything would go back to normal of its own volition, or (2) become overnight Christians, grab a bible, and start praying. As far as choices went, they were both pretty terrible.

"I'm not going anywhere, am I?" not-quite-Bill asked dejectedly. "This is it for me."

"Don't talk like that," Ted said. "There must be something we can do." But there wasn't, and he knew it.

"You could do something," not-quite-Bill said, just as a tiny *plunk* sounded in the water beneath him.

"Anything, Bill," Edith said, stroking his chubby shoulder.

"You couldn't knock me up a peanut-butter sandwich, could you?" not-quite-Bill asked imploringly. "Thank you, ma'am."

"Are you sure that's a good idea?" Ted asked. "I mean, you're already sitting on the toilet. Do we really want to tempt fate?"

Gripping both sides of the bowl, not-quite-Bill grit his teeth and grunted, "If you don't mind, I'll have some peanut butter sandwiches and a couple of bananas, and if you tell me no, then so help me God I'll start singing again!"

Edith rushed out the door and down the steps, the sound of her footfalls followed by the clattering of plates and the refrigerator door opening and slamming shut. It wasn't but a minute later before she'd returned.

"Here you go, Bill," Edith said. She was carrying a stack of sandwiches tall enough to play *Jenga* with. Setting the plate on the edge of the sink, she slowly took a step back, nervously anticipating his next move.

"I'm not an animal, you know," he said, gesturing to his fat, naked body. "A little privacy wouldn't go amiss, uh-huh."

"Of course," Edith said. "I'll go and finish my puzzle. Ted?"

Frankly, Ted didn't know what to do. He knew that leaving not-quite-Bill to his own devices was probably a bad idea, and yet the very sight of him, seated on the commode like a shaved grizzly, prompted Ted to reconsider. "Okay, but I want you to shout if you feel something happ—"

"Oh, dear, he's *dead* isn't he?" Edith gasped. The fact that not-quite-Bill had slumped forward, face-first, into the sandwiches – there were worse cushions to have when your time came – seemed to answer her question well enough. Sinking to the floor beside him, she sobbed and wailed until the man on the toilet no longer looked like Fried Banana Elvis, nor late 60s Elvis or even black-and-white Elvis.

It looks like Dad, Ted thought. And it was. Gone were the ridiculous sideburns, the quiff, and the quivering lip that made him look as though he were in the throes of a perpetual stroke. His silver hair – what was left of it – had returned, and the red, bulbous nose suggesting a youthful fondness for liquor was back as well, squashed onto his face in the manner of a drive-by tomato shooting.

"Oh, this is *horrible*," Edith blubbered.

Ted hugged her. "It's okay, Mum. Dad's in a better place now."

"No," she said. "I mean, look at all those wasted sandwiches..."

36

Geoff and Barry – or Jake and Elwood, since they'd donned black hats and shades – had somehow managed to bounce the majority of undead Knickers patrons either out the door and back into death. It was easy if you knew how; all you had to do was wait for them to get close enough, and one swift hook to the side of the head was usually enough to knock it clean off. The zombies were pretty useless without it; all that remained were confused bodies, bumping into shit, tripping over shit... it reminded Geoff (Jake) of the days he worked down at the clinic, handing out methadone to zombies of a different type.

"You've got one on your ten," Geoff remarked casually.

Barry, who'd been busy cleaning up the few remaining zombies *with* heads, turned around and said, "Yeah, I see 'im... Hey, that's no zombie!"

And it wasn't. It was some skinny, Jheri-curled pimp in a red leather jacket, moonwalking back and forth while periodically pausing to kick his leg about, as if trying to shake off a recalcitrant spider.

"Shamone! Shamone! Check-da-mone, WHOOOO!!!" he said. "Sham... hey, wait a minute, it's the motherfucking Blues Brothers, Shamone!"

Geoff doffed his hat and whipped it at him, taking his cue from that little fella, Oddjob, from the James Bond films. Turns out it only works if the brim is razor sharp, however; the fedora simply bounced off the pimp's shoulder, as useless as a pair of tits on a tropical fish.

"Y'all know how *rude* that is?" Leroy admonished him, kicking the hat across the room and executing a perfect 720 degree spin. "Shamone!" he screamed, grabbing his crotch. The invisible spider had surely reached his nuts by now.

"Elwood, take him out!" Geoff yelled. A headless zombie had latched itself onto his back, riding him bareback as if his name were Seabiscuit.

Barry (Elwood) lunged at the pimp, who countered with a dainty little sidestep. Momentum carried the burly bouncer-cum-Blues-Brother forward, sending him somersaulting over the bar top.

He landed hard on his back, knocking the wind right out of him. It didn't help that he'd also hit a beer bottle ass-first, its neck having ripped through the seat of his trousers and... *entering* him. It hurt like hell, but presently he was too distracted by the strange man back there with him to let it over-bother him much.

"Oh, I know you!" Barry grunted, extracting the bottle from his anus with an audible *pop*. "You're that mad professor... What's your name again?" He snapped fingers repeatedly, the way certain idiots do when they're trying to recall something they probably never even knew in the first place. "*Hawkins*, ain't it?" he said. "*Simon* fucking Hawkins!"

Not quite, but close enough. Professor Hawking nodded in response with his eyes.

"What are you still doing here? Don't tell me. Your minders fucked off and left you to fend for yourself. Bastards. There ought to be a law against leaving your disabled clients to fight off zombies on their own. Broken Britain, that's what it is, mate. I blame the credit crunch."

Just then, the professor's eyes rolled back into their sockets, and a steady BEEP, BEEP, BEEP began to emanate from... wait, was that coming from inside his *head*?

"What's that noise?" Barry asked, but the professor was no longer paying him any attention. "Hey, mate, your head's beeping. Just thought I'd let you know. I mean, that might be something you need to get looked at... and it's getting louder and faster, too..."

Stephen Hawking, CH CBE FRS FRSA, physicist, cosmologist, author of *A Brief History of Time* and *Fifty Shades of Relativity*, had suddenly become a ticking time-bomb.

I knew it was a good idea to install that self-destruct trigger, he thought, as the red digits on his retinas counted down from ten... nine... eight... seven...

"Mate, you've got numbers in your eyes," Barry said, taking a closer look. "That can't be right, can it? I mean, I know you're practically a cyborg already and whatnot, but..."

He'd begun counting along now; it was hard not to.

Three... two...

"Oh, I get it," Barry said. "You've made a bomb out of y—"

37

The rooftop of Knickers was blown sky high, raining bricks and mortar upon the unsuspecting town. If you'd have looked up a moment or two after the blast – though doing so would've seared your eyes and the rest of your face as well – you just might've seen the smoke and flames parting as something ethereal passed through them. The Pit-Dweller had been stealthy thus far in its assault on Bellbrook, keeping mostly to itself, but it was amazing how quickly all subtlety went out the window when your ass was on fire.

Down on the street, the people fled in droves, trying to get as far away from ground zero as possible.

"What the hell just happened back there?" Marcia gasped, panting. A large chunk of brick landed several feet away, leaving a dent in the pavement. "And the first person to mention aliens is gonna get a kick in the nethers."

Clarence shut his mouth before he could speak. So what if he believed aliens were responsible? He also believed that the majority of his charm emanated from his crackers. Without them, he'd be powerless.

"We need to get off the street," Goth Girl said. If it wasn't for her pasty white face, they wouldn't have known she was there in the dark. "We're asking for trouble out here. Whatever's going on, we need to lay low until it's over."

"Who died and put *BLECH* Siouxsie Sioux in charge?" Drunk Boy demanded to know. He was cantering along just behind, bouncing off walls, shop frontages, and anything else he stumbled into.

"Screw you, pisshead," Goth Girl said. "If you've got a better idea, now would be the time to say."

"Love, I haven't even got a clue where I am..." he mused. A long strand of frothy drool dangled from his chin, finally breaking off and splatting on his shoe. "I'm shurprished I'm shtill alive after what all I've had ta drink tonight..."

Just then, the giant letter 'K' from the Knickers marquee fell from the sky, crushing Drunk Boy into the ground. 0.92% BAC sprayed out in all directions, coating the cobblestones with his boozy blood. It was all very horrible and, Marcia thought, horror film cliché.

Goth Girl was just about to scream when a dark, morose voice inside her head interrupted:

Really? After all these years?

It was true; everyone knows that Goths don't scream. If you're lucky, you might get a disgusted grunt, or a sickened whine, but on the whole it ran against everything they stood for. Goth Girl opted for a pitiless grumble on this occasion. The warm blood dripping down her cheek suggested that she might've been just a little callous.

"Quick, everyone in here!" Clarence said, booting open the door to a nearby laundrette. "Before we all get taken out by giant letters..."

"Did anyone see where those three lads went?" Marcia asked, glancing over her shoulder. "I could have sworn they were right behind us when we left the club."

"I'll bet they went up with the roof, when the club exploded," Goth Girl said. "One minute they were there, and the next... well, probably three streets away, at any rate."

"Can't help them now," Marcia sighed, following Clarence in through the splintered door. For a moment she didn't realise what she was doing. Then it hit her:

I was looking at his ass...

Not looking... really looking, like I wanted to grab it. God I love him. He's so handsome and perfect and I just want to bite his...

"Are you okay?"

Marcia glanced up to find Goth Girl staring at her as if she'd just compared Cradle of Filth to a steaming pile of elephant dung.

"Yeah, I think..." Marcia lied. *If by 'okay' you mean,* "were you just dreaming about fucking Clarence, the man whom you loathe more than anyone else at work," *then yes, yes I'm quite okay. I may be sick in the head, apparently, but...*

"We need to call someone," Clarence said, pulling his mobile from his pocket. He jabbed at the buttons – as if trying to bring the trusty Nokia 3210 to orgasm – before realising it was all a bit pointless. "Doesn't seem to be a signal. Shit! Shit! Shit!"

"Never mind, honey," Marcia said. The words left her mouth before she'd had a chance to filter them. "I mean, never mind... it's probably just... well, the explosion..." *Why did I just call him honey? Why, for the love of God and all that's good and pure, do I just wanna SING to him right now; something by Whitney Houston or, heaven help me, Justin Bieber?*

Confused, Clarence said, "Yeah, it *was* pretty big, wasn't it?"

I'll bet YOURS is pretty big, you handsome bag of fuckable.

"I think I need to lie down," Marcia said. "I'm not thinking straight..."

"That's lesbians for you," Clarence sighed. "If only more of them *thought* straight!"

Marcia made her way across the laundrette, swiping an empty box of Ariel™ (because if you want it *really* clean, you need ground-up mermaid bits) off the top of a machine and clambering up onto it. Her head had been flooded with song lyrics for some reason, each verse sappier than the one before it. It was as if Stevie Wonder, Luther Vandross, and Celine Dion had decided to have a *ménage à trois* between her ears, and it hurt like a sonofabitch. People say that childbirth is the most painful thing a woman can experience, but they'd never had to listen to the theme from *Titanic* mashed up with Nat King Cole's 'When I Fall in Love' and several other torch songs all at once. A fusion of such piteous potency, it was almost enough to drive Marcia insane.

Mercifully, a distant rumble interrupted this swirl of sickening sentimentality she'd been sucked into, shaking the very ground where they stood. Several boxes of Persil went tumbling over the edge of the abandoned machines as Marcia snapped out of it.

"What the hell is going *on* out there?" Goth Girl asked. "Is this the apocalypse or what?" Being a Goth, she had to resist getting overly excited at the prospect; it probably *wasn't* the End of Days, after all, and Satan probably wasn't coming with his minions (Hitler, Hussein and Thatcher) to finally destroy the world once and for all.

Still, *something* was happening. Bellbrook was clearly going to hell in a hand basket, and as Marcia lay back on the washers with images of Leonardo DiCaprio and Kate Winslett swimming through her head, she couldn't help wondering whether hell might be a preferable alternative.

38

"What the fuck is it!?" Lee spat, tugging at the impossibly long hairs now sprouting from his chin. "I've never had a beard before in all my life, and now suddenly I've got one down past my bollocks!"

Alfie watched in terror as his own beard continued to grow. "This shit ain't normal…" he said. "It just keeps getting longer!"

Poor Calvin, who couldn't speak clearly at the best of times, thought to add, "I c-c-can't b-b-believe t-t-this is h-h-happening." His own beard was down to his ankles already. "I t-think w-we're z-z-z-z…"

"Z-z-z-z-*what*?!" Lee yelled at him. "Just spit it out already!"

"Z-z-z-ZZ Top!"

"Don't be ridiculous!" Alfie said, standing on his beard now, repeatedly throwing his head back in a vain attempt to tear it off.

"Calvin's right!" Lee said. "My dad has – *had* – all their records. I remember the album covers; dudes with silly beards and guitars." He wound his five-foot beard around his hand. "Ours look exactly like theirs, only longer."

"I *do* feel the sudden urge to find a guitar…" Alfie said. "And a sharp outfit," he thought to add.

"Hang on," Lee said, as if remembering something important. "Only *two* of the guys in ZZ Top had beards; the other one didn't." He turned just in time to witness Calvin's beard fall out, as if on cue, cast off like a discarded costume piece.

A look of relief washed over Calvin's face as his beard piled up at his feet. "W-well, I g-guess I'm the b-baldie t-then," he said, rubbing his freshly shorn chin in disbelief.

"We need to find some scissors," Alfie said, pulling his beard into a long French plait. "These things are gonna keep growing until they bury us completely; we'll *suffocate* if we don't do something about them soon!"

"Curl up and die!" Lee suddenly blurted out.

Alfie looked shocked. "That's not the attitude to have..."

"No, you dickhead. *CURL UP AND DYE*. It's a hairdresser's just down the street. We'll be able to lose our beards there for sure! Hopefully they'll stop growing if we wax them from the roots."

"G-good thinking," Calvin said. "D-do I h-have to come with y-you? I m-mean, I'm the b-baldie ch-chin, remember?"

"We're in this together," Alfie said. "And we don't know what might happen if we split up. Have ZZ Top ever split up before?"

"Fuck knows," Lee said. "Come on, I can hardly breathe as it is."

Along the way, they passed a dog groomer's called *SHORT BARK AND SIDES*, a clothiers for midgets called *DO YOU HAVE THIS IN A SMALL?*, and a glaziers called *A PAIN IN THE GLASS*.

"There it is!" Lee said, pointing down Victoria Street to their destination. "We'll be rid of these beards in no ti—"

That was as far as he got before being vaporized. Before his friends knew what happened, they too were overtaken by the the blinding white light. It was as if none of them had ever existed at all. Nothing remained, not even a Croc.

And it was all the Council's fault, too, for it was them that approved the grant allowing CURL UP AND DYE to be built in the first place, even though it was essentially on the outskirts of Bellbrook, and not officially part of town. If anything, it belonged to Renford, two miles over, but the mayor was loath to incorporate it due to his brother owning and operating CROPS AND BOBBERS, Renford's own premier hair salon.

39

Sharon Conker screeched, long and shrill upon the night. At her prompt, dogs in the neighbouring villages and towns began howling at the wildly oscillating moon, which was apparently still confused as to whether it should be quarter, half or full thanks to Leroy and his *Thriller* shenanigans.

"Calm down," Clive the Cameraman said. "Screaming isn't going to help, is it?"

"Calm fucking *down*?" she shrieked. "Look at me, Clive. Take a good, hard look at me and tell me what you see!"

The thing was, Clive had been looking at her since they'd escaped the carnage of Knickers Nightclub. If anything, it was impossible *not* to look. He'd never seen anything like it in his life. On the plus side, his mixed feelings for Sharon had finally been put to bed. I mean, how could he possibly fancy her *now*? Now that she looked like... "Freddie Mercury," he said. "But that doesn't necessarily mean you're going to *stay* that way. You might—"

"I might *what*, Clive?" she sobbed. His gaze fell to the ground, like a berated child who'd been caught stealing sweets. "Turn into David Bowie? Do a little duet with myself? Why the fuck have I grown a moustache? What have I done to deserve this? And why in the blazes do I have 'Radio Ga Ga' stuck my head?"

"Look on the bright side," Clive consoled her. "Could be stuck with *Lady* GaGa instead. And anyway, remember that song? All you *need* is Radio Ga Ga."

"Are you trying to wind me up, you little shit?" she said, putting her hands on her hips. With her new moustache and teeth, it was impossible for Clive to take her seriously. "This isn't normal. Something... attacked me in there. Something I couldn't *see*. I feel like I've been violated by a poltergeist!"

Having seen a few of Sharon's previous boyfriends, Clive had to wonder whether molestation by a supernatural entity would've been such a bad thing. "I didn't see anything," he mumbled.

"Of course you didn't!" Sharon shot back. "If poltergeists were visible, they'd just be people! Angry people throwing things around and raping at will."

"Look," Clive said, "that's all well and good, but it still doesn't explain why you're Freddie Mercury now all of a sudden." It was dark out there in the street, and all this talk of rape-y ghosts was *not* helping to alleviate his fears. "Something attacked you – so you say – and now you're the resurrected frontman of one of the greatest rock bands in the history of mankind. Does that sound like a normal Friday night out to you?"

Sharon shook her head. *Normal* Friday nights usually involved copious amounts of vodka, a tumble in the bathroom of some squalid club, and then on to Ken's Tuck-In Fried Chicken for a three-piece with a side of coleslaw. This whole Freddie Mercury thing was decidedly new territory for her.

"And what about the zombies and that Michael Jackson pimp?" Sharon said, recalling the horrors they had just witnessed. "If it hadn't been for those Blues Brother bouncers, we'd be having our innards gnawed out by now."

"This makes absolutely no sense," Clive agreed, "but standing here talking about it isn't going to help. We need to find someone who actually knows what the bloody hell is going on."

On they walked into the night. Arriving at the centre of town, they found the square deader than a eunuch orgy. The wind was kicking up an almighty fuss, but apart from that, all was still amongst the abandoned cars and food stalls.

"Looks like the whole town's off," Clive said, gawping at the deserted street.

"Only the ones stupid enough to be out this late," Sharon muttered darkly. "Do you think any of those…" She didn't want to say it, but needed must. "…*Thriller* zombies survived the explosion?"

Clive sighed. "I don't think *anything* survived that," he said. "I wonder what set it off, anyhow?"

"No matter," Sharon said, "the show must go on." She immediately slapped a hand over her mouth. "I didn't mean it like *that*!" Her eyes grew wide with fear. "Holy shit, I think I'm going slightly mad! I go crazy… erm… it's a kind of magic, or something! Fuck, Clive, don't just stand ther—"

His hand connected with her cheek harder than he'd intended, but she was obviously cracking up; that didn't make him a woman-beater, did it? "Pull yourself together!" he shouted, avoiding eye-contact with her. She looked as though she were about to tear his head clean off and use his spine as a backscratcher.

"You hit me..." she whispered. "You nearly knocked my bloody moustache off!"

"Sorry, I didn't know what else to do; you kept making all these Queen references, and I'm scared shitless that the rapergeist is coming for me next!"

Just then, a number 15 bus appeared at the end of the street, rolling along as if its driver hadn't a care in the world.

"It's coming this way," Clive said. "The driver might be able to help us."

"Save me... Save me... Saaaaaaaaave meeeeeee," Sharon sang at the top of her voice, its range and power uncharacteristically impressive. Just that morning in the shower, she'd sounded like two injured cats mating on a mattress of broken springs; now, she sounded like she was ready to hunt down Brian May and have another crack at it...

The bus pulled up, hissing loudly as its air brakes released pressure. The door rattled open, and out stepped a man dressed as a Native American, followed closely by a cowboy and a construction worker.

"Thanks, but we'll wait for the next one," Clive said, eyeing the three strange men suspiciously.

"We nicked it," the cowboy admitted, gesturing to the bus behind them. "Had to; gotta find some people out here tonight."

Sharon twiddled her moustache between her thumb and forefinger, in the manner of a Victorian detective considering a particularly tricky case. Realising what she was doing, she quickly dropped her arm. "What's going on?" she asked the men before her. "Is this the world we created?"

The cowboy shot her a confused look in reply.

"It's okay," Clive said. "She's transmogrified into Freddie Mercury and keeps blurting out song titles. I'm assuming that once she's run out of those we all recognise, she'll move onto the lesser-known ones."

"Wow, Freddie Mercury, huh?" the Native American said. He held up his hand, palm out. "How!"

"We don't know," Clive said. "She just *did*."

"No, he was greeting h..." the construction worker said, trailing off. "Never mind. You wouldn't happen to be a GI, would you?"

Clive shook his head. "I'm a cameraman for Channel 5," he said. "And it's no good asking her what she does; she'll most likely tell you she's a fat-bottomed girl from Barcelona."

"Oh well," the cowboy said, climbing back into the bus. "Hope you figure out what's happened to your friend, though to be honest, things have been a bit crazy for everyone tonight. I wouldn't expect any answers. Besides, that moustache is rather fetching. Might want to see a dentist, though."

"*Hang* on," Sharon said, flabbergasted. Clive was about to interject when she cast him a glance that said, *Don't stop me now!* "You can't *leave* us out here like this. Have some staying power!"

"Was that a Queen song?" the Native American asked, following the cowboy onto the bus. "I don't remember it."

"Well, if I knew what a fucking bohemian rhapsody was, I might've used that one instead!" Glancing past the Native American, Sharon couldn't help noticing that the bus looked nice and warm inside, and a hell of a lot safer than where they were presently standing. "Look, we were down the road at Knickers when it was attacked by zombies, of all things, right before the whole place went sky high. You wouldn't be able to give us a lift back to the studio, would you? Out here we're in the lap of the gods..."

"That one I remember," The Native American said. "I've got two questions for you. First of all, where is your studio, and secondly, will there be a GI there, and possibly a guy dressed in leather?"

Sharon didn't want to lie, but a little white one couldn't hurt, would it? "If it's men dressed in leather you're after, a TV studio would be the best place to find them."

From the driver's seat, the cowboy shouted, "Yee-haw! All aboard, pardners!"

"Thank you, you crazy people," Sharon said. "Come on, Clive. We'll be safe back at Channel 5."

Clive shrugged. At the end of the day, it was him who'd have to explain what Freddie Mercury was doing at the studio. *I could say it's a lookalike*, said a sceptical voice inside his head. *Just someone I'm dropping off at the* Stars in Their Eyes *set.*

"What have we got to lose?" he said, following Freddie/Sharon onto the bus.

40

I'm a punk! I'm a punk! I'm a... well, I used to be a highly respected general practitioner, but not anymore. Nope. Gone are the days of writing prescriptions and signing notes for indolent wankers who'd rather drink than work all day. Gone are the days of telling little Billy Bloom that the bump on the tip of his penis is really nothing to worry about, but we'll have to lance it just the same. Gone are the—

"Wha'choo doing out so late?" came a voice from Lucius Cain's left, derailing his train of thought. "Y'all shouldn't be walkin' the streets. It ain't safe, motherlicker!"

Lucius turned to find a massive, bipedal creature standing between two parked cars. He couldn't tell if the cars were just small – like those ones you can buy nowadays that fit down the side alley – or if the shadowy figure looming over them had been terrorizing villagers while running a side business in beanstalk development.

Either way, the giant spelled trouble.

"Who the fuck are you?" Lucius asked, quickly slapping a hand over his mouth. In forty years as a GP, he'd always wanted to tell his patients what he *really* thought; that it was just a cold, so go home and man the fuck up; that if you didn't want to be sore in your basement, you should really stop having sex with diseased vermin; that no matter what your mother says, masturbation does not cause blindness and that the poor old dear is just scared of catching you in the act whilst watching some documentary about hillbilly duck-wranglers. Forty years on and he'd never so much as said 'boo' to a goose, and now, here he was, standing before a creature large enough to hammer him into the ground, and his mouth – *I trusted you! We've been together since the start!* – had finally betrayed him.

"Who the fuck am *I*?" the giant said, stepping forth from the shadows. Shit, he was a lot bigger than his silhouette gave him credit for. "I'm Snoop fucking Diggity. You wanna go toe-to-toe, bitch?"

Do I? Lucius asked himself. Thinking about it, he probably *didn't*, but he wished someone could tell his mouth that. "Yer damn fuckin' right I do," he said. "I eat punk-ass gangster rappers for breakfast." *No, no, no, no, I didn't mean that! What I meant to say was, please don't hit me, sir.*

The giant reached down and hooked his hands beneath the cars on either side of him, effortlessly flipping them over. It was an amazing feat of brute strength; one that Lucius knew, if he wanted to be taken seriously, he would have to match.

No fucking cars my side, he thought, scanning the immediate area. There was a bicycle chained to a nearby lamppost, however. Lucius walked over to it, picked up the back wheel, and pulled as hard as he could. The bike clattered against the post and refused to do anything else. "Good job it's tied up," he said, slapping the dirt from his hands.

"I'm gonna rip that safety-pin right outta yo face," Snoop Diggity growled, "and shove it where where the sun don't shine. And then, in about it week, you'll take a shit, and it'll sting like a motherfucker, and you'll remember this night."

Lucius was in no mood to fight, especially not with King Kong's stunt-double. He opened his mouth to apologise, to tell the giant that he was merely an old, confused GP, wandering the streets after a particularly mystifying night. What came out, though, was, "You fucking gangster rappers are all the same. There wouldn't even *be* any rap if it hadn't been for us punks. When was the last time you threw a television set out of a hotel room window?"

"*Today*, bitch," Snoop Diggity said, then added, by way of an inaudible mutter, "but it was only the ground-floor window, and it wasn't so much an entire TV as just the remote. Dead fucking batteries, bitch. Can you believe dat shit?"

"And when was the last time you got really drunk? I mean, so drunk you went out hunting for badgers, and then when you found one, you shaved its eyebrows off?"

"I don't—"

"Or so drunk that you pretended to be pregnant, found a policeman, and then pissed on his helmet?"

"What kind—"

"Yeah, you gangster rappers are all the fucking same. Singing about your money and hoes, how much *bling bling* you got and how many guns you supposedly own. Well, Gigantor, how many guns do *you* own?"

Snoop Diggity reached into his jacket and came out with something Dr. Cain had only ever seen in a museum before. "With this one, I'd say about twenty, maybe thirty."

Lucius gulped. The safety-pin in his face stopped bleeding momentarily as all the blood in his body rushed down to his legs. "That's, erm... that's a very nice musket you have there," he said. "Antique?"

The giant appraised it. "I'd say so, bitch." Pointing its barrel at Lucius, he continued, "I don't know what's gotten into me tonight, but I jus' got this *itch* that can't be scratched..."

"Oh, I'm a doctor," Lucius said. "Maybe I could sort you out with some crea—"

"Not that kind of itch, bitch," Snoop Diggity said. *Wow,* Lucius thought, *he really is good at rhyming.* "I got me an urge to kill stuff," the giant said, just barely managing to cock the musket's tiny flint lock with his fist-sized thumb. "And you, punk, are next." He punctuated his statement with a menacing grin, his golden grill glinting in the moonlight.

Lucius closed his eyes, expecting the musket blast to be the next – and last – thing he heard. So, it came as quite a surprise when he heard an elderly woman's voice instead:

"Timothy, you put that gun down right this instant!"

Timothy?

Lucius opened his eyes. She was marching up the street with that look about her; an expression suggesting you'd be a fool to engage her in light banter, and an even bigger muppet to discuss the week's politics. Whoever she was, Snoop Diggity was afraid of her. The rapper took a step back, lowering the musket as ordered. His eyes became doleful, as if this dear, little old woman with a face like thunder was capable of knocking him out with one solitary blow to the temple.

"Mama, I wasn't gonna shoot nothin'," Snoop Diggity lied. "I was just showing the punk my antique."

She walked up to the giant and slapped him, hard as you like, right across the face. What was funny was the little hop she had to perform in order to reach. "What have I tole you, boy, about callin' people names?"

"But Mama, he *is* a punk."

She jumped up and slapped him again, this time on the opposite cheek. "You'd better apologise to that man right now, boy, or you ain't recordin' no songs with DJ Bizzle and MC Rizzle for a week, do you hear me?"

While they were arguing, Lucius took a step back, and another, then another, and before they knew it he'd managed to slip away. "I almost got shot," he muttered to himself, strolling swiftly down a side street. It wasn't quite true. To get shot, first you would need a functioning gun (which the musket wasn't), and you would also need an assailant with fingers small enough to fit through the trigger-guard (which Snoop Diggity didn't have). If anything, the most dangerous thing about that whole scenario had been the giant's livid mother.

"Fucking mums are fucking mad!"

Lunging out into the road, Lucius kicked a brick through the front window of Burns and Stiffs' Funeral Home.

If he'd perhaps looked both ways, like his mother always taught him, he might have seen the bus careening toward him at sixty miles per hour. But he hadn't, and the last thing he heard was a meaty *pop* – like a sausage being pricked – as his body made way for seven tonnes of steel.

41

Ted didn't know where he was going, or what he would do when he got there. He'd spent the last half-hour trying to convince his mother that not-quite-Bill wouldn't come back as Zombie Elvis, and yet she'd *still* insisted on barricading the bathroom door just in case. Maybe she was right. Maybe he *would* come back as Zombie Elvis; stranger things had already happened tonight, beginning with his foregone fish-finger tea.

"What the *hell* is going on?" Ted cried at the moon, which insisted on changing phases every few seconds. Somewhere out in the night, he heard the hiss of air brakes, like a bus coming to an abrupt stop. There was a tang in the air, of smoke, of *barbecue* almost. Somebody was having a cookout, he guessed, but he'd never smelt meat like *that* before.

Walking along the dark, desolate street, Ted thought about the peculiar circumstances by which his father had met his fate, about the way the phone lines had suddenly went down, about Doctor Cain showing up with fat in his hair and a safety-pin through his nose – God, he'd regret that in the morning...

He thought about how his mother had reacted to not-quite-Bill's body, perched there on the toilet with a face full of peanut-butter sandwiches. How she'd cried for almost three whole minutes before going back to her baked-beans puzzle and "a nice glass of sherry to calm me down."

But that hadn't been the end of it. Not that he thought it would be. When his mother started singing Patsy Cline songs at the top of her voice, Ted knew he had to do something.

Anything...

By and by, he began to encounter people even more confused than himself out on the street. Apparently, there'd been a massive explosion at a local nightclub. That, Ted thought, would explain the scent of burning flesh at least.

"D'you know where Tulsa is?" asked a small man with a singed noggin and wonky spectacles as he rushed up to Ted.

Ted recoiled from the lunatic. "I'm no geography teacher," he said, "but I believe it's in Oklahoma..."

The still-smouldering man checked his watch, like this had some bearing on the whereabouts of the American city.

"Twenty-four hours," he said, hopping from one foot to the other as if he were standing on hot coals. "I'm only... twenty-four hours from Tulsa," the man sang. It was at this point that Ted bid the maniac adieu and walked in the opposite direction.

The street became filled with them; people singing, dancing, climbing onto cars and removing clothes and swinging body parts that should never be swung in public. It was a very carnival atmosphere, just without the carnival. Everyone in town had apparently been infected – affected – by whatever had changed his father.

If that's the case, Ted thought, then why not me? *Why am I the only...*

His thoughts trailed off as the sudden, overwhelming urge to dress himself all in leather struck him like a nine-pound hammer.

Turning back to the Gene Pitney fella, who'd taken to singing about how something had gotten hold of his heart, Ted said, "Hey mate, I told you where Tulsa was. Now it's your turn."

The man stopped dancing and smiled. "What are you after?"

"Leather," Ted said. "The campest leather I can get my grubby little mitts on."

42

"Holy shit!" Sharon Conker said, making her way up the aisle to the front of the bus. "Did you just hit somebody?"

McLoud, the cowboy, shook his head and flicked on the windscreen wipers. Blood and brains smeared left and right across the glass, a tell-tale safety pin slowly sinking out of sight. "I don't think so."

"Then what's all that red stuff?" Sharon asked. "And is that a *finger*?"

It was indeed a finger, caught beneath one wiper, tracing its final fuck-yous upon the windscreen.

"So I *hit* someone," the cowboy sighed. "He came out of nowhere. I've never driven a bus before. There was something gritty in my eye."

"All very good excuses," Clive the Cameraman said, "but nothing they will take into consideration when it goes to trial."

"Look, can we get a wriggle on," Kavannah said, shifting nervously in his seat. "It's going to be getting light in a few hours, and we haven't even completed our line-up yet."

"Whatever," Freddie/Sharon said. "Who wants to live forever, anyway?"

"Okay, buckle up!" McLoud said, putting the bus in drive. "Does anyone know any good songs?"

43

"Is she *dead*?" Clarence asked. "If she's dead, I've got to get out of here. I don't like being around corpses at the best of times. Now that I've seen them dancing and feasting on brains, I like it even less."

"I'm not dead," Marcia said, pushing herself up into sitting position. "I'm just... *extremely* fucking horny, and strangely attracted to you right now." She didn't know where it came from either, but it was best to just let it all out, be honest about it. What was the point in trying to control something so powerful, something so natural and carnal? It was like trying to tell Paul Potts that three burgers was plenty, and did he *really* need the fourth and fifth.

"What?" Clarence gasped. "Now I *know* you're dead... or maybe *I* died... am I dead? Is this heaven?" He looked terrified. "I was too young to go. I haven't even finished paying for my X-Box yet. I've never even once slept with twins!"

Goth Girl lit a cigarette and grinned. "This is getting *very* interesting," she said, exhaling smoke from between her black, glossy lips. "Methinks one of you is infected." The way she put it – playfully, and not in the least bit bothered – made the whole episode even more surreal.

"There's something about the way you look tonight," Marcia said, seductively slinking across the laundrette – if indeed such a thing were possible. "Can you feel it? Can you feel..." – she hissed, licking her lips as if she'd just finished a bag of donuts – "...the *love* tonight?"

Goth Girl almost choked on a lungful of smoke.

"But... but you're a lesbian," Clarence said, taking a step back, as if Marcia was not a woman at all, but a crocodile, or a giant praying mantis, or Madonna.

"I was playing hard to get," Marcia said, almost slipping in a puddle of spilt soap. "Everything I do (I do it for you)."

"Did she just speak in brackets?" Goth Girl asked. "Is that even fucking possible?"

"Apparently," Clarence said. "Look, Marcia, this isn't *you*. You've been taken over by the aliens, and they've infected you with... whatever it is they're using. You don't love me, or fancy me, because you're a *lesbian*, and I'm cool with that."

"You're the first, the last, my everything," Marcia continued, "the wind beneath my wings, the best a man can get. Nothing compares 2 U. I want you to want me."

"Now she's talking in numbers..." Goth Girl said, clearly impressed.

"She's talking out of her arsehole," Clarence said, sliding along a wall of washing machines.

"First time ever I saw your face, it must have been love." She wriggled her hips, as if this would somehow sway

Clarence's decision to just give up the goods. "Tell me what you see, here and now, no, don't speak; love will keep us together, even though you don't bring me flowers." She sighed. A tear fell from the corner of her eye and slowly rolled down her cheek. "I can't make you love me, but I just want you to know one thing. That I would do anything for love (but I won't do that)."

Clarence relaxed. It sounded like she was done for now. "Look, Marcia, you're ill. You've got the alien in you. You've been through... wait, hang on; when you say you won't do *that*, what exactly do you mean?"

"What?" asked Marcia.

"You said you would do anything for love, but not *that*. I've always wondered what *that* thing is."

"Anal?" Goth Girl said. "I mean, I'd do anal, but some people wouldn't, and personally I've never seen Meat Loaf as a fan of it."

"I don't think he wrote a song about *not* doing anal," Clarence said. "Surely it would be a given that many people wouldn't do it. If the song had been called, 'I Would do Anything for Love (*Including* That)', then it might make more sense. No, he had to have been talking about something else..."

"His sister?" Goth Girl suggested.

"Yeah, that *kinda* makes more sense," Clarence said. "I mean, incest is a problem at the best of times, but the woman in the video didn't look like his sister. I imagine Meat Loaf's sister to be relatively well-built for some reason."

"Does it matter?" Marcia asked. "You're the one that I want...ooh...oooh, ooh."

"Is she going to keep going on this all night?" Goth Girl said. "Only, I don't think I can take it..."

Just then, the launderette door flew open. It hadn't occurred to any of them that locking it might be a good idea.

"Look, I don't want any trouble," the man said, stepping over the threshold. "I just need to check the dry-cleaning for any leather items."

<h2 style="text-align:center">44</h2>

Everything was going according to plan. Better than that, even. These people were *idiots* when they got the music in them. The Pit-Dweller would have given itself a nice pat on the back if it had hands, or even a back to pat in the first place.

Down below, Bellbrook was on fire; people were running naked through the streets, singing at the tops of their beautifully pained voices. It had watched as a group of death-metal fans burned the local church before hanging themselves from a tree in the adjacent cemetery. It had seen rival street-dancers pummel each other into oblivion. It had witnessed an elderly woman climb to the top of the library – *bring 'em back or we'll break your legs* – where she'd managed four full minutes of unbridled yodelling before a disgruntled owl came along and knocked her off her perch. It had observed the local policemen partake in a spirited drag race to the tune of 'Greased Lightning'. It had seen children (who should have been in bed, in all fairness) taught to pickpocket by some bearded vagabond, who then sang into the faces of their mortified victims.

It was all too good to be true; pity it would soon be at an end. There couldn't be *that* many left down there, after all, scurrying about like rats in a musical maze. Still, it wasn't over yet. Plenty more enjoyment to be had before sun-up.

45

"What's going on out there?" Clarence asked the newcomer, who (true to his word) didn't seem the least bit interested in anything besides the piles of dry-cleaning in back. "Are there zombies? Is that Michael Jackson pimp still alive?"

"I have no idea what you're talking about," Ted replied, rifling through a pile of soiled garments. "All I know is that my dad is dead, my mom is Patsy Cline, and I really need to find some... aha!" He held up the leather catsuit. "Reckon I could fit into this?"

"Not a chance," Goth Girl said. "You should have shaved your chest before you came out the house."

Ted looked deflated, emotionally if not physically. "I'll have you know that this body packs down quite nicely. Why, I once managed to squeeze into a 34" waist! Granted, that was back when I was more like a 36"..."

Looking at him, Clarence would have put him closer to a 50" now.

"Well," Ted said, "I'm going to try this on, anyway." Glancing past Clarence, he thought to add, "Why's that woman looking at you like she wants to eat you?"

Clarence turned to find Marcia straddling one of the clothes dryers, sucking her finger and eye-balling him as if he were an ice cream sundae and his penis was the cherry on top. "Shit, it's getting worse..." he said.

"What's getting worse?" asked Ted.

Clarence turned back to him, averting his eyes as the man attempted to squeeze his substantial bulk into what was essentially a leather body sock. "This! The aliens!" he cried. "This whole bloody nightmare is getting worse! She's over there looking at me like I'm some sort of all-you-can-eat buffet, you're over here looking like Shamu in a bin-bag, and Goth Girl over there—"

"What *about* me?" she said, folding her arms like a petulant child.

"Well, you're a Goth. Isn't that *enough*?"

She nodded in agreement. "Yeah, but you don't have to be so mean about it."

"Oh my God, you're totally *right*!" Ted said, half-in and half-out of his new leather suit. "This isn't right at all. I watched my father die tonight, sitting on the toilet. He was Elvis Presley. He'd gone from black-and-white Elvis to fried banana Elvis in less than three hours. That's not right in a million years, is it?"

"Sounds like you've been through the wringer, too," Clarence said. "Elvis, you say?"

Ted thought back to his father sitting on the loo, his old self returning, the quiff shrivelling up and disintegrating like an autumn leaf. "Yeah, which was odd because he was always more of a Beatles fan. Never had much time for Elvis; said he couldn't be doing with all that groin thrusting and lip twitching." He sighed. "I figured he'd been possessed at first, but when I started thinking about it, I remembered reading that demons seldom alter their host's appearance. They creep in, like evil ninjas, and they can do a lot more damage with their host in human form than they can with horns poking out the tops of their heads. Plus, it's hard being stealthy when you can't get from one side of the kitchen to the other without clip-clopping. It's the *hooves*, you see."

Goth Girl shook her head. "This is all very interesting," she said, "but do you have any idea what's going on out there? Something must have happened; something must have *changed*."

"Aliens," Clarence asserted, probably for the twentieth time that night. "I'm sure of it."

Across the room, Marcia slid down from the dryer. "He's so smart," she said, trying to be seductive and failing miserably. It was like watching Sharon Stone after several shots of Sambuca; you *should* find it attractive, but for some reason it's just really embarrassing.

"Hang on a flipping minute!" Ted said, suddenly forgetting all about the mess of leather he'd become entangled in. "The LP harvest!"

"You mean the record cull?" Clarence asked.

"Call it what you want," Ted said, "but it *has* to have something to do with what's happening." He slapped himself in the forehead. "Gah, I'm so stupid! Why didn't I think of this sooner?"

"Because you're so stupid?" Goth Girl suggested, as she lit up another cigarette.

"It all makes sense now," Ted said. "Well, in a fashion. I mean, everything that's happening out there is somehow related to music, right?"

"That would explain the Michael Jackson pimp and his stable of *Thriller* zombies," Clarence said. "It might also explain why my colleague over there suddenly wants to ride me like Kauto Star, and why you're suddenly set on slipping into the most ridiculous costume since Halle Berry played Catwoman."

Ted looked down at his rotund body and the leather catsuit covering barely half of it. For a split-second he realised how daft he must look. It was a fleeting thought, however, and after it had passed he reapplied himself to making the meagre, slim-fitting garment fit properly (as if this were even possible).

"I think I know what it is," Ted said, shoving around his rolls of fat. "I was at the landfill earlier today, dumping off the last of the records. I heard the workers talking about some sort of underground building they'd discovered. When I asked their foreman what was going on, he said it was nothing, just some old foundations that had been unearthed."

"Ancient burial ground," Goth Girl said, exhaling another fantastic plume of smoke. After it had cleared a little, she continued, "Like in that film with the girl that gets sucked into the TV, or the one where they bury their cat and the thing comes back all fucking nasty."

"But how could they have not known it was there?" Clarence asked. "I mean, would they actually dig a landfill on something so sacred?"

"This is the Bellbrook *Council* we're talking about," Ted said. "They'd dig a landfill beneath your grandmother if she stood still long enough. Maybe they did know about it. Maybe they just stumbled upon it by accident, but either way they've fucked us good, wouldn't you say?"

Marcia, who'd been listening from across the room (when Al Green wasn't keeping her pacified), suddenly stepped forward. Clarence jumped back, genuinely frightened of her by this point. It was funny, Marcia thought, how the tables had turned. Just earlier that day, she'd been standing at her desk, waiting for the office to clear out so she could leave. He'd popped over to lay on the sleaze, and *now look at him. Look at him quiver...*

"Do you think we can stop it?" Marcia asked, rubbing her temples with her fingers; it hurt just to think straight, what with all saccharine *love* crap and Streisand warbling in the background. Whatever was projecting the music into her mind, it must have set this shit on shuffle. "I mean, how far is this landfill? We could be the *four little angels of peace.*" She sang this last bit, then slapped herself in the face for surrendering control so easily.

"It's about a mile away," Ted said, "I don't suppose any of you has a car?"

"Nope," Clarence said.

"I'm a Goth," Goth Girl said. "We only like hearses and ice-cream trucks."

"So we're walking," Marcia said.

Ted shrugged. "We might be the only chance Bellbrook has. Something evil has taken over this town. It's true what they say: eventually, the rhythm *is* gonna get you."

He'd finally managed to squeeze into the tight leather outfit (most of him, anyway). After giving himself a once-over in the mirror – not bad if you could get past the unsightly bulges – he turned to the rest of the survivors, took up a nearby mop handle, and said, "Let's take this thing down before it destroys us all." And then, as they nervously filed out the door and into the street, he added, "If anyone happens to spot a cowboy, a Native American, a GI and a construction worker, let me know."

46

Across the street, in the doorway of a boarded-up shop, four vagrants argued in Scouse accents over which one of them was Ringo. It turned out that none of them wanted to own up to it, and so a quarrel had broken out.

"We can't all be John," one of the men said.

"Why not?" said another. "It worked for Spartacus."

"Look, we all just need to decide," said a third. "I'm John, Steve's Paul, Roger's George, and you, Mike, can be Ringo."

Mike wasn't happy with the nomination one bit. "That's fucking ridiculous," he said. "I'd rather be Pete Best than fucking Ringo."

"Well you *can't* be Pete Best," the one called Steve said. "You're Ringo. Nobody even remembers who Pete Best was. Ask *anyone*. Ask them who's Pete Best and I'll bet they tell you he's an alcoholic footballer."

"And Ringo's only known for his work on *Thomas the Tank Engine*," Mike said. "So, no! I'm Pete Best, and that's that."

"Look, this isn't a debate," Roger said. "Just accept your places and... oh, shit – hang on gang, here comes trouble."

Just then, a second group of men came a' sauntering down the street. Their leader moved like some sort of simian, pouting his lips and clapping his hands as they went along. His gesticulations came to an abrupt stop, however, when he noticed the four men standing in the doorway. "Well, look at what we have here," he said, placing his hands on his hips as he leaned to one side. "It's The Beatles. Pleased to meet you... hope you guess my name."

"Jagger," Ringo sighed. "We don't want any trouble, so why don't you lot just jog on, huh?"

Mick Jagger – he of the bee-stung lips – feigned surprise, turning around to address his gang. "They want us to jog on," he said, snorting. Turning back to their rivals, he sneered, "What's the matter, *Beatles*? Scared we're going to steal your thunder?"

"You don't frighten us, Jagger," George said. "Coming around here like you own the fucking place. Why don't you go paint a door black and leave us the fuck alone?"

Jagger was incensed by the insult, seeming to grow several inches in height; years of strutting around like a Neanderthal had disguised his true stature. "I'm not having any of that," he said, licking his abnormally large lips. "Here's one you might appreciate, though, Beatles. We're all going to come together, right now, over ME!!!"

Throwing back his head, Jagger roared like something from a Ray Harryhausen film and then inhaled forcefully, sucking in tepid night air. The Beatles became terrified as the vortex hit them, and they realised he wasn't joking around.

"He... he's sucking us in!" Ringo screamed.

"Grab hold of something!" George cried. "His lips will smother us to death!"

But it was no good. The four vagabonds failed to find their grip, and within seconds they were just a mess of limbs, kicking and flailing between Jagger's mighty lips. The whole thing lasted no more than twenty seconds, but to a casual observer it would've easily been the best show the Stones had put on in quite some time.

When the limbs stopped moving and the Liverpudlian screams abated, Jagger finally spat them out. The four Beatles landed on the pavement in a twisted heap, broken, sodden, and motionless, and just a wee bit sorrier than Miley Cyrus on a wreckingball.

"Come on, boys," Jagger said, wetting his parched lips. "I've heard The Bay City Rollers are knocking about..."

47

Three cars sat idling at the traffic light on Bellbrook ring road. Engines roared as the drivers pushed down on their respective accelerators, gunning for a quick start. When those red lights turned green, they would be off and away, tearing up the night – and the tarmac – on their way to first-place glory. At least, that was the plan. The only problem was that Marc Bolan, Falco, and Eddie Cochran weren't exactly known for their driving prowess.

Bolan stole a quick glance at his competition before steeling his eyes on the road ahead. "Bring it on, you bastards," he said, casually flicking a cigarette out the window. Or, at least he *would* have flicked it out the window, if said window had been wound down. Instead, the butt bounced back into his lap, burning a hole in the crotch of his flares. He shrieked in pain – fitting how much he sounded like a wounded T-Rex – as he dug around for the red-hot butt beneath him. By the time he found it, wound down the window, and properly flicked it out, the light had already turned green. He looked up just in time to catch the tail lights of Falco and Cochran, the two of them peeling off into the distance.

Luckily for Bolan, though, they didn't keep their lead for long. From out of nowhere, a massive fuel-tanker came barrelling around the corner and careened across the lanes, taking out both racers in an explosion that wouldn't have looked out of place in one of Michael Bay's wettest, wildest dreams.

"Hahaaaargghhh!" Bolan cried, pounding the steering wheel with both hands. "That means I've *won*, doesn't it? I'm the *winner*!" He had no idea who he was talking to, not that it mattered. Seconds later, what appeared to be Beth Ditto fell from the sky, crushing both him and his car into something marginally flatter than a postage stamp.

48

O'Brian climbed out of the car, breathless and flustered. The playing cards had been fun while they lasted, but he needed something *more* to get him off. Besides, apart from one Joker and a six of diamonds, the rest of the cards were all soggier than a week-old cornflake. He'd been frantically masturbating for nearly four hours now, to no avail. Every time he came close to finishing, something else popped into his head and ruined it for him. *Grandmother's face, an old INXS tune, that purple fucking dinosaur the kids love so much...*

He squeezed his sore penis, giving it a gentle tug through his trousers. "We'll find us something," he said. "Oh, we'll sort you out yet, little buddy."

But how?

He knew that if he didn't get it out of his system soon, he'd likely implode. He'd read articles, in those magazines you find in dentist waiting rooms, that claimed leaving one in the pipe was incredibly dangerous. If *Men's Health* said it was bad, then who was he to argue?

Just then, a little voice in the back of his head whispered two magic words:

Autoerotic asphyxiation...

"What's that?" O'Brian asked, scratching his head and also his balls.

You've got to wrap a belt around your neck and wank yourself to death!

"Oh, that sounds a bit... *dangerous*," he said, frowning. "Does it have to be all the way to death, or can I just go until I'm kinda close to death?"

Nope. Has to be to death, I'm afraid. On the bright side, at least you'll go out on a high note.

"Yeah, but on the dark side, some fucker's gonna find me with my dick in my hand, swinging from a tree."

Yeah, I could see why that might be a concern, the voice continued. *Well, you could try cutting off just before death, but I'm not promising anything. A lot of people have tried and failed.*

With thoughts of David Carradine and Michael Hutchence in his head, O'Brian bravely undid his belt and pulled it through the loops. *In for a penny, in for a pound.*

Wandering of into a nearby park, he chose the closest tree. An owl perched upon a high bough, going *hoot, hoooot,* which, if O'Brian had understood owl, would've translated to, *You're not really going to masturbate yourself to death, are you? You daft prick!*

Luckily, the tree boasted a branch that was low enough for him to reach. O'Brian hadn't fancied climbing; he wasn't as young as he used to be, and the last time he'd tried to climb a tree, he'd ended up in A&E with broken ribs and several inches of oak inside him.

He looped the belt over the branch and tied it. There was just enough slack remaining to wrap around his neck, which he took advantage of while frantically stroking his throbbing shaft. Once he had everything in place, he slowly dropped down from his tip-toes, intensifying all sensations as the belt grew tight around his neck. He saw colours that he'd never seen before, and the only sound he could hear was the steady rush of blood between his ears; that, and the dratted owl overhead, still doing its level best to spoil his epic wank.

After about thirty seconds of this, O'Brian had to admit that things weren't going quite as expected. He was still no closer to orgasm, and the belt had dug so deeply into his neck, his airway had been closed almost completely.

"Caghhhaghh..." he rasped, clawing at his makeshift noose with one hand. It was wound too tight; he couldn't get his fingers beneath the strap.

Told you so, the owl said, its voice echoing down from impossibly high above. Not that O'Brian could've understood it anyway; owlese hadn't been a foreign-language option when he'd gone to school, not like now, where you could choose between anything from French to German, Klingon to Meerkat...

Suddenly, his mind flooded with lewd images; the playing cards, the prostitute who'd deserted him earlier, watching his grandmother in the shower, those damned Pussycat Dolls, three fifths of Take That, Susan Boyle (for some reason), and anyone from ABBA who didn't have a beard...

That did it. O'Brian came – and *went* – at exactly the same moment, gurgling his death rattles as he swung in the breeze, all the while being berated by one very bemused owl.

49

On their long trek over to the landfill, the group managed to avoid confrontation for the most part, but none of them had anticipated running into the entire cast of *West Side Story* about halfway there. There had been stabbings and maulings as Sharks and Jets did battle all along Cooper Street, but as traumatic as the experience had been for the Ted, Marcia, Clarence, and even Goth Girl, it was damn near impossible to take knife-fights all that seriously when their participants insisted on singing and dancing the whole bloody time.

"This the place?" Clarence asked, looking out over the abandoned worksite.

"Yeah," Ted replied. "The landfill is over there, just past that digger." He chafed against the leather bunching up in his hairy ass crack. "I just hope they haven't started filling it in yet... don't much fancy the thought of having to unearth the thing all over again."

"Whatever we do, we need to make it quick," Goth Girl said, pointing to Marcia, who was presently trying to lick Clarence's face.

"Come on, then," Ted said, leading the way. "We need to put an end to this before..." He trailed off in mid sentence as the unmistakable horns sounded in his head, tapping his foot to the infectious disco beat that followed.

"Come on, man!" Marcia said, dragging him along as she resisted the urge to dry hump his thick, meaty leg.

Moments later they'd reached the pit, staring down into its dark, ominous depths. The night had grown tempestuous, shreds of tattered paper and polystyrene borne along upon the winds. Somewhere off in the distance, an owl hooted. Ted wasn't sure, but he could've sworn it said: *Serves you right, you pervy old bastard!* Whatever that might have meant.

"I'm not going down there," Goth Girl said, taking a step back from the yawning chasm. "There aren't many things I'm afraid of, but lowering myself down into a pit of pure evil, to face something we might not be able to beat, just happens to be one of them."

Clarence nodded. "I'm with her," he said. You could practically see the yellow of his skin glowing in the moonlight. "I know I said I'd be glad to help, and I have, really, if you think about it—"

"How, exactly, have you helped?" Ted asked, resisting his own urge to flee for the nearest YMCA.

"What about back there," Ted protested, "when you were about to get battered by those three women dressed as Mexicans squawking 'America' at the tops of their lungs? Did I not pull them off you? Did I not stab one of them in the face with her own stiletto?"

"Yeah, you leave him alone," Marcia said, stroking Clarence's arm. "You'd be *dead* if it wasn't for my Clarence. *Dead*, I tell you."

Clarence flinched at her insinuation; he'd never been anyone's *anything* before. Under different circumstances, it might have felt nice, but... "Look," he said, "take Marcia with you. If you need any help, she's pretty handy. Not afraid to get her hands dirty, that one."

Marcia looked shocked. "You're just trying to get rid of me," she said. "Don't throw your love away, Clarence. My heart is broken."

"Look, if you really loved me," Clarence said, knowing that she didn't but using it against her anyway, "then you'd go down there with Ted and save the fucking day!"

"I would do anything for love," she said, nodding her affirmation. "Even that."

"We don't have time for this," Ted said, bravely stepping up to the edge of the pit. Visions of not-quite-Bill passed through his mind; it seemed so long ago, and yet two hours back he'd still been alive. Not right, but alive. "I'm going to end this, with or without your help."

With that, he started down into the hole, a fat man in a tight leather suit with nothing left to lose.

"I'll prove my love to you," Marcia said, pulling Clarence close to her. "In everything I say and in all I do."

"Better get a move on then," he replied, giving her a not-so-gentle nudge. "You don't want to be on your own down there." She flailed her arms in a vain attempt to keep her balance, but it was no use. "I'll see you when you make it back up," he said, waving goodbye.

She waved back to him as she fell down into the pit.

"For you, my looooooooooooooooo..."

"What a fucking nightmare..." Clarence mumbled, but Goth Girl was too preoccupied painting her nails to reply.

50

"This isn't the way to the studio," Clive the Cameraman said, taking in their unfamiliar surroundings. "Where are we going, and why are those people dressed as animals?"

He was right. They were nowhere near Channel 5; in fact, they were going in the total opposite direction. He was also right about the people that had fallen in with the bus in the meantime, lumbering along on all fours, hemming them in on either side. They weren't just dressed as animals, though...

Somehow they had morphed into something *between* animal and human. Primate faces peeked out from within lush lions' manes. Pairs of human legs bore along giraffes and zebras, looking like something out of a parade. A fat lady was swinging a skinny lady from her face; it was the most rudimentary impression of an elephant any one of them had ever seen, and yet so *convincing*...

"Listen!" Kavannah said, cupping an ear as he slid down one of the windows. "Is that—"

"The Lion Sleeps Tonight," said Sid, the Native American, nodding his head to the rhythm. "I used to *love* this song when I was a kid."

Just then, a hippo – four men joined together by lord knows what – slammed into the side of the bus, knocking its occupants from their seats. From the back, Freddie/Sharon cried, "Where's Flash? Ahaahhhhhh! Saviour of the universe."

"I don't like this song anymore..." the Native American said, staggering to his feet. "And can someone *please* watch out for bison, wildebeest, rhinos and other giant creatures on the road?"

"You didn't answer my question," Clive said to McLoud. "Why are we driving *away* from the station? Is there something we should know?"

"Just sit down," the cowboy said. "We'll get you to your precious station soon enough. There's something down this way needs sorting out first."

"And that would be?" Clive asked, grabbing the nearest seat as an entire company of people-parrots collided with one side of the bus, spattering it with blood and feathers. There was a sound – almost a drumroll – as the miniature hybrids bounced off one by one. Several windows cracked, spider-webbing outward from the points of impact, but thankfully none of them were shattered.

The bus continued to protect them... for now.

"We have reason to suspect that one of crew has gotten himself into a spot of bother," McLoud said, "over at the new landfill site." And then, in an accent more befitting his attire, he added, "We're just gonna mosey on down there and rescue our boy."

"Fuck's sake," Clive said, taking a seat near the front. "If we don't get butchered by Baloo and his fucking friends out there first..."

The cowboy simply shrugged, tipped his hat, and began to whistle the theme from *Rawhide*.

51

"Magnificent..." the Pit-Dweller said, awestruck by the madness below.

The residents of Bellbrook were now transforming into animals, while others remained in human form, becoming prey for the myriad predators on the loose. Croco-people hunted children; bear-men and wolf-women chased terrified townsfolk through the streets, howling and growling to a tune only the moon could fully appreciate.

"Absolutely magnificent..."

Down the Pit-Dweller swooped, trawling its tendrils through anyone and anything in its path. People shrieked and squealed as they were eaten alive by man-igators and tiger-ladies, but they shrieked and squealed even louder when the Pit-Dweller gushed through them like a Friday night vindaloo, turning them into the very things they sought to escape.

"Look, up there!" one man screamed, and for a moment the Pit-Dweller thought it had been spotted. Had it not be stealthy enough? Human faces turned to the sky, to where a dragon flapped its mighty wings.

"It's PUFF!!!" a delirious woman yelled.

"How *dare* you!" the Pit-Dweller roared, before realising they were talking about the giant green dragon soaring towards them. "Oh, yes, *that*! Yeah, it's puff..." *Whatever the fuck that means...*

The dragon swooped low, spewing fire over anyone foolish enough to remain in the street. As the flames died down, leaving charred human statues in various states of repose, the dragon shot up into the sky and disappeared into its darkness.

This is just too much fun, the Pit-Dweller thought. Dragons, hybrid beasts, people still singing as if the end of the world (*their* world, at least) were something to celebrate. And maybe it *was* something to celebrate; maybe these sad, pathetic souls despised their pointless little lives so much, death would prove a welcome reprieve.

The Pit-Dweller laughed heartily – like Santa Claus or Brian Blessed – as the chaos continued to unfold. On the far horizon, a creamy glow heralded the coming dawn. No matter; these idiots would be killing one another long into the next day, and the day after, and the—

Only something wasn't right.

It was that feeling you get when you *think* you're alone in the house, but something goes *bump* in the other room. No longer so interested in the carnage on the streets below, the Pit-Dweller knew it was time to return to its sepulchre. Someone was there. Somebody was trying to play the hero by crashing its party.

Over my dead body, the Pit-Dweller thought, shooting high into the sky and knocking one magic dragon straight into orbit.

52

"What does it look like in there?" Marcia asked, keeping her distance. The first thing she'd learnt as a newspaper reporter was: never stick your head into a particle accelerator.

Of course, this was no particle accelerator, but it was close enough for the rule to still apply. For all they knew, peeking through that door would leave your head trapped within some prehistoric multiverse, while your errant arse-end remained back in the landfill. And who knew what would happen then? Perhaps your head would simply fall off, get gobbled up by a passing pterodactyl, leaving your body stumbling blind in a pit lined with old LPs, wondering *what the fuck just happened* for the rest of all eternity.

"Too dark to tell," Ted said, turning back to face her. Marcia was glad to hear it, not least because he still had a face. "I don't suppose you've got a torch or a lighter, have you?"

Marcia sighed and patted her pockets. "When I came out this evening, I didn't expect to be trawling through some ancient crypt with some guy I just met."

"Is that a no?"

Marcia nodded. "That's a no." She looked up to the rim of the pit, and was just about to call for Goth Girl – where there's smoke, there's fire – when suddenly there came a tiny *click* from within the structure before them. A great, blinding light spilled out into the landfill, illuminating thousands of garish record sleeves previously hidden in the darkness.

"Found the switch," Ted said, his eyes quickly adjusting. "Who would've thought something so old would run on 40 watt screw-ins?"

"Not me," Marcia replied, peering in through the door.

Given the trajectory of their evening thus far, she wasn't that shocked to find heaps of human bones, lampshades fashioned from face leather, curtains made of stomach lining, and rudimentary clay bowls brimming with all variety of vile offerings. With places like this, these things were to be expected part and parcel. Granted, the property owners would likely struggle to sell it, but when you had a skeleton sofa, upgrading to something more refined – a four-bed semi in Dartford, for instance – was usually the furthest thing from your mind.

"This looks like the place," Ted said, stepping over the threshold. "Honks a bit, but that's to be expected when your carpet is evidently black pudding..."

"I'd say a demon lives here," Marcia said, following him in. "Either that, or a teenager with a crap taxidermy hobby."

"You believe in *demons*?" Ted asked, slightly taken aback.

"After what's happened here tonight, is it even possible to *not* believe in demons?"

Together they entered the catacomb, Ted leading the way. The smell reminded him of earlier that afternoon, when he'd walked into CARTER & CARTER'S OLDEN DAY BULLSHIT. There was that same tang in the air, of things long untouched, of objects dustier than a politician's truth-stick, of primal relics unearthed by hapless work crews or dug up in some uppity git's back garden.

"Look," Ted said, pointing to a dark cavern in the far wall. "I've got a feeling that whatever we're looking for... it's down there." He self-consciously adjusted his leathers, covering an exposed nipple. *Wouldn't want to look silly, now, would we?*

"After you," Marcia said. While Ted was busy inspecting the cavern's entrance, she'd picked up a large bone, taking practice swings like Babe Ruth. "Hey," she said, allowing the makeshift club to fall to her side. "We're just like Riggs and Murtaugh. Cagney and Lacey. Batman and Wonder Woman."

"More like Thelma and Louise," Ted added. "Or Bonnie and Clyde, the way we're heading..."

Pressing on into the cavern, they soon found themselves lost in a system of narrow, winding tunnels. The light from the entrance chamber only illuminated their path so far, and it wasn't long before they were walking in near total darkness, Marcia clinging to Ted's flabby arm to avoid getting separated.

Ted concentrated on their surroundings, making mental notes as they moved along. *Already been down there, been down that one, been there, ooh, this is a new one... oh, no, I remember it now, it's the one shaped like a question-mark...*

"This place is amazing," Marcia whispered, wishing she had a camera, or at least a notepad and pen.

"Yeah," Ted agreed, "I'll bet they said the same thing about King Tut's crypt, just before they all started choking on chicken bones and falling off of scaffolding."

"I miss Clarence," Marcia whined. "I hope he's okay."

"Of course he's okay," Ted said. *God, leather really does chafe.* "He's up there with the rising sun. Oh, and by the way, you do realise that you're only having feelings for him because of... well, whatever *this* is. He doesn't love you. He told me that you're actually a lesbian. A *muffer*, he called it."

Marcia sniggered. "I was just putting him on when I told him that; playing hard to get."

"Well, it worked," Ted said. "Trust me, when this is all over, you'll go right back to despising him. Everything will return to how it was." But it wouldn't, would it? Not for him, anyway; his father was dead. Not-quite-Bill wouldn't be coming back to life, now would he? No, this wasn't some bedtime fairy-tale, where everything turned out fine in the end. There would be no *happily-ever-after*, not this time.

"What's that?" Marcia gasped, pointing to the faint glimmer of light up ahead.

Ted grimaced at the thought. "That, m'dear, is probably where we both die horrible deaths. You up for it?"

I'll never see Clarence again. I'll never hold him, touch him, or sniff his hair when he's not looking. I'll never be able to grab his ass and then point to someone else as if it were them and not me. I'll never see his face – oh, such a beautiful face – again, or the way his eyebrows knit together when he frowns. I'll never...

"Just answer the fucking question already," Ted groaned. "We haven't got all night."

"Sure," she replied, steeling her resolve. "Let's go."

Approaching the mysterious light like two people approaching a wounded tiger, or an off-duty lap-dancer, neither one of them wanted to lead the charge, slowly creeping forward side by side instead. They both knew that whatever lie ahead, it would change their lives forever, that this night would soon be over, and that a lot of people were counting on them to do the right thing, whatever that was.

Reaching the end of the dark, dingy corridor, they discovered some kind of stone portal, left slightly ajar.

53

They're in my fucking room! the Pit-Dweller thought. Visions of people rifling through its knicker drawer, stumbling upon its collection of ancient pornography – *Roman Chicks, Greek on Greek, Fun Times in Bethlehem* – caused its ethereal hackles to rise. *Gotta get back quick, before they find my dild—*

54

Candles flickered along a wall made entirely of bones and teeth. The chamber was, Ted thought, exactly what Dorothy Draper might have come up with if her client requested something grotesque, unlivable, and offensive enough to keep even the Nazis away.

"Reminds me of my first bedsit," Marcia said. "At least I put a few posters up to hide the damp."

"I seriously doubt that whatever dwells down here has time for posters," Ted said. "Where would it get blu-tack from, to start wi—"

His observation was interrupted by Marcia's sudden shriek. The noise had been so unexpected, he nearly spun around to strike at its source on reflex. When he saw what she was looking at, however, he nearly shrieked himself.

In the darkest corner of the room, farthest from the dim glow of the candlelight, there sat a grotesque figure upon a throne. Centuries of snot and drool had solidified on its chin, forming pitch-black stalactites which hung from its gaping maw. Its eyes were distinctly reptilian, as if its Mum had had a thing for serpents, and its large, flared out nostrils were wide enough to stick a fist inside. Its rippling, scaly flesh had been completely mummified, gnarled, black and dry.

"Is that... is *that* what's causing this?" Marcia said, her hand clamped over her mouth.

"Seems like a pretty good assumption to me," Ted said, stepping closer to the desiccated beast. "Whatever it is, it's not of this world, and certainly not of Bellbrook. I haven't seen anything *this* ugly since that David Icke sex tape."

"But what *is* it?"

"It's a tape in which David Icke got his balls licked by a—"

"No," Marcia gasped, raising a tremulous finger to the thing in the corner. "What is *that*! Was my Clarence right? Is it the aliens after all?"

"I've never seen an alien like this before..."

"Seen many aliens, have you?" Her sarcasm didn't go unnoticed.

"I've seen enough YouTube videos to know that this isn't an alien. It must be some sort of... *demon*."

"Ah, *demons*," she said. "Of course it is. How stupid of me. Here I was thinking it was E fucking T." She fell silent as Ted leaned in closer to the... demon/mutant/alien/thing. "You're not going to *kiss* it, are you? Because that would be a little weird for me."

Ignoring her, Ted reached for the shiny bauble hanging from the mummy's sinewy neck. He'd never seen anything like it before, and yet he could sense that it was... *important*, somehow.

"This pendant," Ted said, turning it over in his hand. He could feel the energy within, tingling his fingers. "This is what gives it life."

"Well, whip it off, then," Marcia said, "and let's get a wriggle on. I'd rather drink soup from one of Noddy Holder's platform shoes than spend another minute down here."

She was right. Ted too felt the urge to get out, to resurface, to breathe deeply of the dawn air and put this whole debacle behind him. He clenched the strange pendant in his fist and pulled.

55

The Pit-Dweller faltered and fell the last few metres to the ground. It was bad enough there were people down in its lair, mucking about with its private belongings, but now they'd gotten a hold of its pendant, and that just wasn't cricket!

As it crashed into the earth like a drunken Superman, a great cloud of dirt and debris flew up into the brightening sky. If there had been a loud *thump* upon its emergency landing, the Pit-Dweller hadn't heard it. It had been too busy going, *fuck me, fuck me, this is going to hurt,* to hear much of anything else.

Clambering up onto its massive, gnarled haunches, the ancient beast dusted itself off as it rose to its full eighteen feet of height. It was then that it realised it was no longer invisible, it astral form swiftly fading from the physical plane.

"What the fuck?" it said, noticing the two people staring at it from the pit's rim. It wanted to say something smart – *take a picture, it'll last longer* – but nothing came.

Not quite true.

A bus came barrelling toward it, sailing over the edge of pit. As it whirled around to face its doom, it was met with seven tonnes of steel and a cowboy behind the wheel. The Pit-Dweller could've sworn it heard the driver scream, "Yippee ki-yay, motherfucker," but when something that heavy slams into your chest at sixty miles per hour, it's difficult to remember all the details.

Crushed beneath the weight of the Bellbrook number 15, both of them far off their regular routes by this point, darkness overtook the Pit-Dweller as it uttered its final curse.

56

"So, if you think about it," Marcia said, stepping out into the morning light, "we're all just bald monkeys, and..." She abruptly trailed off, spotting the wrecked bus and the smouldering heap of flesh and bone beneath it.

"Is that—"

"—the *demon*?" Ted gasped, suddenly feeling very exposed. "I'd imagine so. What the fuck happened to it?"

"Great big bloody bus came through and killed it," a voiced called out from above. It was Clarence. "Came out of nowhere and slammed right into the cunt!"

"Well, talk about luck..." Marcia said to Ted. "Do you think it was coming after us?"

Ted shrugged in response. "Do you feel any different?" he asked.

She looked up at Clarence and wished he was within punching distance. "I think everything's going to be *juuust* fine," she said.

"I just want to get out of these silly leathers," Ted said, already peeling them off as they started back up the hill.

"Can you at least wait until we find you a proper change of clothes?"

57

Many were the dead, and many were those left permanently scarred by the experience. Michael J. Fox had never been more grateful for his parents' strict curfew, and Stephen Hawking had finally found some use for his self-destruction mechanism. Then there were those unfortunate half-men, half-beasts that had not quite returned to their human forms, but the townsfolk found a place for them soon enough – the Bellbrook Hybrid Zoo opened on November 21st, in a ribbon cutting ceremony officiated by Professor Brian Cox himself.

Following a brief celebratory dance with the rest of The Village People (he didn't want to, but they'd insisted, and he was already dressed for it anyway), Ted returned home to find his father still dead, but at least his mother had finally finished her godforsaken baked-bean puzzle. After a few weeks of mourning, they both moved on with their lives. Ted became Leather Guy full-time, forming a tribute band with Sid, Kavannah, and McLoud called *The YMCA-ers*. Edith Butcher eventually remarried, and though Bobby Graceland would never replace his father, he would serve as a constant reminder of what had happened that fateful night in Bellbrook.

After much deliberation, Marcia took the job offered to her by Channel 5. Her show with Sharon Conker – *Martin & Conker Investigate* – proved to be such a ratings hit that both of them went on to live lavish and leisurely lives, despite continuing to hate each other with a passion.

Snoop Diggity was offered a three-record deal with Jay Z's Roc-A-Fella-Records, but at his mother's insistence, he was unfortunately forced to decline. He now works the night-shift at Bellbrook's premier sandwich-shop, *The Sub Shack*.

Life went on and the world kept turning, which was fortunate for everyone on board. As for the Pit-Dweller, that demon of dance, that beast of beats, well... should you ever happen to find yourself in Bellbrook, walking past our Hard Rock Café, take a little look up.

No, not that one; that's Meat Loaf.

Nope; that's Bonnie Tyler.

Between those two... there it is.

Without music, life would be a mistake.
– Frederick Nietzsche

Thy milkshake brings all the boys to the yard
– William Shakespeare

ADAM MILLARD

VINYL DESTINATION